"WHAT DO YOU WANT?"

The maid nervously curtseyed to the court magician. "I need a charm, Lord Medron. A powerful charm against a witch."

"You must tell me who this witch is and why you fear her."

"*Him,*" the maid said. "Alaric the minstrel. He's bewitched my Lady to love him."

Medron shrugged. "This is nothing but the way of young people."

"So I thought. But the boy is hardly a fit lover for my Lady. He came upstairs and I left them alone together. But I could see them through a chink in the wall. When I was sure that . . . I locked the door and called his Majesty immediately, then returned to watch. As the King entered the sitting room, making a great deal of noise, I saw the boy . . . I saw the boy fly out the window! I didn't dare tell till I got a charm from you."

"This is a serious charge you bring. Come, I will make you a charm, and in the morning we will bring this matter before the King. . . ."

"Very well done . . . the best fantasy novel I've read this year."
—Jerry Pournelle, author of *Janissaries*

Born to Exile

Phyllis Eisenstein

A SIGNET BOOK

NEW AMERICAN LIBRARY

A DIVISION OF PENGUIN BOOKS USA INC.

Portions of this novel appeared originally in issues of the *Magazine
of Fantasy and Science Fiction*.

Originally published by Arkham House Publishers, Inc.

SIGNET, SIGNET CLASSIC, MENTOR, ONYX, PLUME,
MERIDIAN and NAL BOOKS are published by New American
Library, a division of Penguin Books, USA Inc., 1633 Broadway, New
York, New York 10019

First Signet Printing, November, 1989

1 2 3 4 5 6 7 8 9

PRINTED IN THE UNITED STATES OF AMERICA

To Alex,
without whose support
this book
could never have been written

Born to Exile

THE SUN OF ALARIC'S FIFTEENTH SUMMER BEAT down on his head as he stared at the moat, the drawbridge, and the broad walls of Castle Royale. A dusty wind swirled around him, adding another layer of grime to his dark, travel-stained clothes and drying the rivulets of sweat on his face and neck. He shifted his knapsack with a shrug, and the lute that was strapped to it twanged softly.

Presently a man in light armor came out of the shack on the near side of the bridge and glared at the boy from under an enormous, beetle-browed helmet. He held a broadsword at ready. "Identify yourself."

Alaric swept off his peaked black cap and bowed as much as his pack permitted. "My name is Alaric, and by trade I'm a minstrel. Having been advised by many that my songs are worthy, I come to offer them to His Majesty and, in short, to become a hanger-on at court."

The guard grunted. "What weapons do you carry?"

Alaric's slender fingers touched his worn leather belt. "None but a paltry dagger, useful for carving fowl and bread. And the feather in my cap, for tickling my enemies to death."

"Empty your pack on the ground and give me that stringed thing."

While Alaric demonstrated that the pack held noth-

ing but a brown cloak, a gray shirt, and four extra lute
strings, the guard examined the lute. He shook it,
peered into it, rapped it with his knuckles. At last,
satisfied that it was nothing dangerous, he returned it
to its owner and motioned for the boy to repack his
knapsack.

"Gunter!" he shouted. A second man, seeming, in
his identically patterned armor, to be a twin to the
first, appeared from the shack. "Take him inside to
the Great Hall. He seems to be a jester, even if he says
he's a minstrel. Be sparing of your wit, boy. We already have a jester."

Alaric swung the pack over one shoulder, the lute
over the other, and followed Gunter across the bridge.
He did not glance back, but in his mind's eye he could
see the twisting, turning road that had brought him to
this place. How many miles it was, he knew not. For
him, it was measured in months, beginning on that
gray day in the Forest of Bedham—eight long months
and tens of thousands of steps carrying him away from
Dall's lonely grave. Eight months through forest and
field, asking directions of peasants in hovels and of
merchants shepherding their caravans of goods to market; eight months in which he was hardly even tempted
to use his witch's power to speed his journey—he
needed a clear and precise knowledge of the location
of his destination for that, and he had none. He
had walked, as normal men did, pretending to be
one of them as Dall had always advised, and he
had finally arrived at Castle Royale, in search of his
fortune.

The minstrel and his escort passed under the portcullis and entered a large courtyard in which a dozen
or so well-muscled, half-naked men were practicing
various forms of personal combat. Alaric's eyes
roamed from swordsmen to wrestlers to boxers, and

he was painfully aware of his own slight physique. Battles were not for his untrained hands. His way was to vanish, as he had vanished from beneath his father's whip.

He was seven that day, the day his mother died and his father revealed the fearful secret: that Alaric had been found on a hillside, a helpless newborn babe clothed only in blood. He was obviously a witch child, for a gory hand, raggedly severed just above the wrist, clutched his ankles in a deathlike grasp. The local peasants were frightened, and some wanted to destroy the infant that was surely a changeling or worse, but barren Mira loved him instantly and took him into her hut. Her husband grumbled sullenly under the lash of Mira's sharp tongue, but he acted the role of father, albeit distastefully, until she died. And then his strong, gnarled fingers reached for the whip.

Alaric, who had practiced his power in secret, flitting imperceptibly from one tree to another in the nearby wood, backed away in terror. As the leather thong slashed toward him, he pictured a particular tree in his mind, complete to the mushrooms that ringed its trunk and clung to its bark. Suddenly, he stood in its shade and the loamy smell of the forest floor filled his nostrils. He never dared return home.

Gunter led the young minstrel toward a side door of the Palace, the largest building inside the fortress. Just before reaching it, they passed a raised wooden platform where an eight- or nine-year-old boy stood alone and unsheltered under the beating sunlight. He was naked but for a loin cloth, his head and wrists were encased in stocks, and his back was covered with raw wounds and clods of dried mud. Tears stood out in stark relief against his dirty cheeks.

"What's that?" Alaric asked his escort.

Gunter glanced back and shrugged. "A page. He misplaced some silver."

"I didn't take it, Master!" the boy whimpered. "I don't know what happened to it, but I didn't take it!"

Pity welled up in Alaric, not for the boy's innocence but for his stupidity in being caught. Theft was an art a youthful vagabond knew well—theft of money, chickens, and laundry—an art that had kept him alive from the day he left home till the night he met Dall, the minstrel with the silver voice. And the silver coins. The money had been tucked under the straw pallet that served as Dall's bed at the Inn of Three Horses. It was easy for an eleven-year-old boy with slender fingers to slip them out in the middle of the night; it was easy for an eleven-year-old boy with a witch's power to vanish to the safety of the forest. But Dall's voice was too compelling, and morning found Alaric waiting eagerly to listen again.

Dall sat in front of the hearth, strumming his twelve-stringed lute and singing lays of ancient times. When he noticed the child, however, he drew him outside. "I'm not going to hurt you," he said in low tones, "so don't be afraid. If you'd like to learn a song or two, I'll be glad to teach you, but first you must give me back my silver. And then you must tell me who you are and how you came by that vanishing trick."

"What?" the boy muttered. "I haven't any silver."

"You have." The man lifted Alaric's chin with his index finger and gazed into the boy's eyes. "I saw you enter my room last night, and I saw you leave. What is your name?"

"Alaric."

"Tell me, Alaric." More than his words, the tone of his voice was the key that opened the boy's lips and heart; his story poured out torrentially, beginning with the discovery of his infant self on the hillside and ending half an hour later with his most recent exploit. At that point, he dug deep in his pockets for Dall's silver and returned the coins with trembling, suddenly shy fingers.

"There is no future in this," Dall said. "No matter how careful you are, you have no eyes in the back of your head; someday an arrow or a knife will find you."

"I've managed so far."

"You've already made your first mistake. Anyone but myself would have raised the cry of witch last night. You'd be an outlaw at this moment, and no one gives shelter to an outlaw, on pain of death."

Alaric hung his head and gnawed at his lower lip. "I thought you were asleep."

Dall plucked pensively at the strings of his lute. "I saw you sitting in the corner yesterday. You spent the whole day watching my fingers. Are you interested enough in the lute to learn to play it yourself?"

"Oh, sir, I'd like that very much!"

"Well then, I happen to need an apprentice. . . ."

And after that, they traveled together.

Here I am, Dall, Alaric thought. *Where you always planned to go when and if the wanderlust left you. It's all just as you said it would be, cobblestone courtyard and all. You used to tell me we'd sing for His Majesty and find our fortunes here.*

Gunter stopped at a watering trough to let Alaric clean some of the dirt off his face and arms, change into his extra shirt, and stuff his ragged cap into the depths of his knapsack. Then, they entered the building that was the Palace proper.

In order to use his power, the minstrel had to be able to visualize his position and his goal, each in relation to the other. Through years of practice—some of them behind Dall's back and against his advice—he had become adept at this. Though other strangers to the Palace might have been hopelessly confused, he was not when, after many twists and branchings, their path gave into an enormous, high-ceilinged hall which was filled with voices and the clatter of dishware.

"Just in time for the midday meal," said Gunter. "The King will want entertainment."

On a dais on the other side of the room sat the King—a big man, still on the near side of forty, blond and ruddy-cheeked, dressed in a gold-encrusted red tunic. He was eating a joint of meat and waving it to punctuate booming sentences. To his left sat a handsome, dark-haired, blue-clad boy, and to his right was the most beautiful girl Alaric had ever seen. She resembled the boy enough to be his sister, but where his features were boldly cut, hers were fine and delicate. Her eyes were wide and green, her nose barely turned up, and her thin lips were perfectly shaped. Her hair, which was very dark, she wore long and caught in a white lace net that allowed curling tendrils to escape its confines and nestle on her shoulders. Her green linen gown clung to a shapely breast and betrayed a narrow waist with the aid of a heavy girdle of chain.

"A minstrel, you say!" boomed the King's hearty voice. "Sit ye down, boy, and give us a song."

"And if it's good, we'll have you for lunch," said the jester, a wiry, big-headed dwarf who wore the traditional motley and bells and sat at the King's feet playing jacks. "And if it's bad, we'll have you for lunch anyway. Fee fi fo fum!" He turned a handspring and wound up on the floor in front of Alaric, looking curiously into the hole of the lute. "Anybody in there?"

"A silver coin lived there once. Maybe he'll come back, if you put in another so he won't be lonely."

"We'll see whether you're worth a coin after you've sung!" The King motioned to a blue-uniformed man behind him, who called for silence in the room.

Alaric's clear tenor rang out with an old, well-loved ballad.

> *"Upon the shore of the Northern Sea*
> *Stands a tower of mystery,*
> *Long abandoned, long alone,*
> *Built of weary desert stone*
> *For a purpose now unknown. . . ."*

Afterward, the King nodded. "I haven't heard that song in years. There was a minstrel who stopped here for a while once and sang that quite well. What was his name?"

"It was Dall, Father," said the girl in green. "Five years ago." She eyed Alaric with half-concealed interest, and when he met her glance she dropped her eyes. She concentrated on a square of green satin in her hands, twisting it and winding it around her fingers as if the action had some use. Alaric was fascinated by the smooth white skin of her hands—untouched by sun, wind, or work—and by her delicate, tapering fingers.

"Ah, yes, Dall," said the King. "He stayed the winter, I remember, and left with the spring thaw. Palace life was too soft for him, I guess."

"He was my teacher," Alaric said.

The King chuckled. "Now I know why you do so well at your trade. He was a master, that fellow. Whatever became of him?"

"He was murdered by bandits eight months ago," Alaric replied.

The princess gasped, then her left hand flew to cover her mouth, and she turned her face away.

The King frowned sympathetically. "Ah, that's a shame. Were the culprits punished?"

Alaric shook his head. "I . . . I wasn't able to catch them." The vivid picture of Dall's scarlet blood splashed over the dry leaves and mold of the forest floor returned once more to haunt him.

"It's hard to watch someone you love die unavenged, I know, lad. But at least his place was taken by someone worthy of it. You're more than welcome here. Join the table." He gestured toward the left side of the hall, where twenty or thirty brightly dressed men were eating. At the movement of his hand, the noise level, temporarily low during and after the song, regained its former height.

Alaric bowed low and went to a vacant seat at one end of a table, preferring the solitude of his own thoughts and an opportunity for observation to the boisterous conversation of the courtiers. Taking wine and beef from two passing stewards, he pretended to be engrossed in eating. Presently, he noticed the jester wandering through the crowd, joking and capering, but coming unmistakably in his direction. With a last cartwheel, the jester was beside him, jarring the bench a trifle with the impact of his small but solid frame.

"What ho, minstrel!"

"What ho, indeed, motley."

"Here's a silver coin," said the jester, holding out one hand. "Now show me its brother."

The youth looked at him quizzically for a moment, then he recognized the reference. "Sorry, that was just a figure of speech. I haven't even a copper in my pocket."

"Tch," said the dwarf. "Here I thought you were slyly hinting that you were a magician as well as a singer."

"Not at all. I can make food disappear, but that's my only conjuring trick."

"Then let me try." The jester's empty hand darted toward the lute that hung over Alaric's shoulder and seemed to pluck a coin from it. "Both for you, from the King, with his invitation to stay until he tires of you."

"*You're* the magician, not I," said Alaric.

"Wrong both ways," the jester replied. "The magician is over *there.*" He pointed across the room to a small, lonely table occupied by a bearded man in long black robes. "That's Medron, said to be a cockatrice in disguise. I believe it. Without the beard, he'd turn his own mother to stone. This trick? Nothing, my boy. Medron can pluck gold coins from the King's mouth." The jester cleared his throat. "As long as he's gotten them from the King's purse beforehand."

"He's *not* a magician?"

"So some would say. Myself, I don't look crosseyed at him. He doesn't have to be a magician to put itching powder in your clothes."

"*My* clothes?"

"What I mean, boy, is that if you *do* know any sleight-of-hand tricks, don't use them. And don't ask me to teach you any. Medron's a *good* wizard. He makes gold out of lead, though I've never seen any of it. But that won't stop him from denouncing you as a witch if he thinks you're competition. And he has lots of little tricks that would convince even *you* of your guilt."

"But the King—"

"Burned three witches last year, just outside the castle walls. Good thing, too. The time before that was inside the courtyard, and the place stank for a week."

Alaric swallowed slowly. "Thanks for the warning. Thanks very much."

"Nothing at all. I like to keep the ship rolling along smoothly. My last message is from the Princess Solinde: she wants you to sing in her sitting room at sundown. Second stairway on the left, three flights up, the door has gilded birds carved into it." He grinned and did a back flip off the bench. "Keep your wits about you," he said as he walked away on his hands. "My grandmother was an owl."

Alaric ate automatically as he watched the dwarf meander back toward the dais, which was now occupied only by the King. The brother and sister had gone.

Toward sunset, blazing torches were scattered around the room, and the twin fireplaces at either end of the hall were loaded up against the approaching chill of night. The courtiers abandoned the tables and clustered around the two hearths, laughing, playing with their huge hunting dogs, and gambling with dice. Alaric plucked idly at his lute for a while, and then he made his way toward the stairway that the jester had indicated. He was stopped at the top of the steps by a blue-uniformed guard who stood beneath a wall-bracketed torch and carried a spear.

"I was invited to sing for the Princess Solinde," Alaric said.

The guard peered into Alaric's knapsack and shook his lute before allowing the boy to walk on, and he pivoted on one foot to watch the minstrel all the way to the door of the carved birds.

Alaric knocked.

The oaken panel swung inward, revealing the beautiful girl and her handsome brother surrounded by giggling, chattering young attendants. The crowd parted in the middle to allow Alaric to enter. He found himself in a small but sumptuously appointed chamber hung with brilliant tapestries depicting opulent, idealized banquet scenes and lit by dozens of large candles hanging in a chandelier. The floor, instead of being strewn with rushes, was covered by an exquisite purple and blue carpet of oval shape and intricate, swirling design. Upholstered chairs of various bright hues were scattered on the rug, and his host and hostess waved Alaric to one of them.

"I am Solinde," said the pale, dark-haired girl. Her lips curved upward in the faintest of smiles—a smile that betokened the poise and confidence of a woman twice her age. "And this is my brother Jeris."

Alaric bowed, not quite certain that he should sit in the presence of royalty, even though the royalty was no older than himself.

"Sit down, sit down," said young Jeris. "You made me tired by standing up all through your song for Father this afternoon." The prince threw himself into the nearest chair, his head resting on one upholstered arm and his legs dangling over the other.

Princess Solinde seated herself on a velvet-covered divan, and the dozen or so young courtiers sank to the floor around her couch. Only then did Alaric perch gingerly on the edge of his chair.

"Dall always sat when he entertained us," said Jeris.

"Did you know him well, Your Highness?" Alaric inquired.

"He was a fine fellow. He used to play hide-and-seek with us, and draughts, and follow-the-leader. We always hoped he'd come back some time.''

"Be quiet, Jeris," said his sister. "The minstrel came to entertain *us*, not we him. Do you know any of Dall's other songs?"

"I know all of them, Your Highness."

"Then play us a happy air."

Alaric complied with the amusing tale of the butcher's wife and the magic bull. While he sang, he noticed that the princess watched him very closely. Her eyes were green, fringed with thick lashes, and they met his boldly now instead of lowering. She looked him up and down until he wondered what she could be searching for.

Jeris whooped at the conclusion of the song, which found the butcher's wife hanging by her heels from the rafters of her husband's shop, waving a cleaver at all the customers. "He never sang us that one, sister. I'll wager he thought it too salty for young children."

"Yes, he did consider us children," she murmured. "Tell us something about his life these last few years."

"How did he die?" Jeris demanded, sitting forward eagerly. "Was it a fair fight, and what were the odds?"

"Oh, Jeris, let's not ask about his death! It's bad enough that he *is* dead; let's not dwell on the circumstances." She glanced around at the young people gathered about her. "Out! All of you out! I wish to speak to this minstrel privately. Not you, Jeris. How would it look to leave me alone with a stranger? My maid Brynit may also stay."

The room emptied as fast as the youngsters could bow or curtsey and flash through the doorway. The last one out closed the door behind himself.

"Tell us now, Master Alaric," the princess said breathlessly, leaning forward in her chair, "was his hair still jet black and his manner proud but kindly?"

"Faugh!" muttered Jeris. "She wishes it were he sitting there instead of you. I shall be sick if you speak of him again in *that* way, Solinde."

"Very well, brother. We shall satisfy your curiosity now and mine at some other time." Daintily, she folded her hands in her lap. "Did he suffer much, Master Alaric?"

"No. It was a broad-bladed hunting arrow, and he bled to death quickly." Alaric remembered too much too well: Bending over the knapsack to count the gleaming coppers won in the marketplace of Bedham Town, his shoulder brushing Dall's as the two of them knelt by the fire. The smell of burning hickory branches that almost covered the lighter scent of the rich, black earth around them. Crickets chirping a mindless chorus. And then, the snick of an arrow being loosed from a longbow somewhere to his left. Alaric vanished reflexively, without thinking, and found himself at their campsite of the previous night, still clutching the knapsack and a handful of coins. He returned to Dall instantly, but it was too late. The gray-feathered shaft had pierced the singer's chest—a shaft aimed at Alaric, that had passed through the space he had suddenly ceased to occupy and struck his friend. Desolated, the boy blamed himself.

"In a sense, it was my fault. The arrow was meant for me, but I moved just before it struck." He felt a tear grow in his eye and petulantly brushed it away. "I'm sorry, Your Highness. I think about it often and bitterly. I loved him as if he were my father."

Solinde sighed and leaned back. "We loved him,

too. And we shall always think of you as part of him.
I'm glad you came to us, Master Alaric.''

"He wanted to return, Your Highness. He spoke of
it often. He never told me why, but I see now that
it must have been because of you and your brother.'' Mentally, he crossed his fingers over that white
lie. Dall had always said that fortune awaited them
at Castle Royale, and now Alaric understood
that he had meant the patronage of the heirs to the
throne.

"That's . . . very good to know,'' she murmured.
"You had better leave now, minstrel; it grows late.''

Alaric stood up and bowed deeply. "Good night,
Your Highnesses,'' he said and backed politely to the
door. As he slipped out and gently shut the heavy
carven panel, he heard a sobbing beyond it and wondered whether it were the princess herself or her little
maid, who had sat silently in the far corner of the salon
throughout the interview.

The guard at the top of the stairs gave him leave to
descend with a curt nod, and when he reached the
main floor and the Great Hall, Alaric found preparations for sleep in progress. Many of the courtiers who
had dined at the long table on the left side of the room
had no private apartments in Castle Royale; they were
solitary knights and minor nobles without retinues
seeking temporary hospitality from their overlord or
desiring audiences with him. A few were pilgrims in
sackcloth, and these huddled close to one fireplace, as
if their very bones were perpetually chilled. A number
of maidservants were moving through the throng with
quilts and blankets, heaping them over cushions or
couches as bedding for the guests. One by one the men
settled down, some with their dogs posted beside them,
some with more congenial bedmates. Alaric found
himself alone with a voluminous, multicolored down-

stuffed comforter; he squeezed into a narrow space near the pilgrims, wrapped himself in the coverlet, and lay down with his knapsack as a pillow and the lute under his protecting arm.

The pilgrims were murmuring to each other in low tones.

"Listen to the wind wail," said a bent-backed old-ster in a coarse, hooded robe. "It's a night for evil."

"It's a night for rain," replied one of his companions, a younger man with a blond mustache and no eyebrows.

"See the flames flicker and blow? The Dark One himself will be out with his witches tonight," insisted the first.

"How many days before we come to the Holy Well?" asked a third companion, a swarthy, grizzled fellow in his fifties.

"Two more, and not soon enough for me. I feel the Darkness creeping up to strangle me."

"We're safe enough here, uncle," said the fourth member of the group, a beardless youth. "They say Lord Medron has powerful spells wound all around this castle, keeping the Dark One always outside."

"I don't know why our good King trusts him. Witches are evil, nephew, every one of them. At night they turn invisible for their foul purposes, and they fly to the ends of the earth for their filthy revels. Darkness oozes from their limbs like honey from a crushed hive."

"I saw nothing oozing from Lord Medron," said the boy.

"After our visit to the Holy Well, perhaps you will see things differently. *My* old eyes know a witch when they see one." He glanced suspiciously around the room, his eyelids narrowed to slits.

Alaric felt every muscle in his body stiffen as the

old man's gaze swept past him. Was there really some
unmistakable visual clue to a witch's identity—the
color of an eye or the tilt of a nose or the thickness of
a brow—that would be apparent to a knowledgeable
observer? Alaric had never noticed anything physically
special about his body, but that might only mean that
he didn't know what to look for. Had that gray-
feathered arrow been loosed at him because he possessed a double handful of coppers or because he was
obviously a witch who could only be destroyed by
stealth and surprise? Would it be best to leave instantly
before anyone recognized the power that he always felt
glowing softly inside him?

"Perhaps the King has a talisman that binds Medron
to his bidding," suggested the grizzled pilgrim.

"Well, our good King is surely a likely person to
possess such," the old man muttered, and then he
launched into an arcane discussion of talismans and
their hypothetical attributes.

Alaric relaxed slowly. The elderly pilgrim had seen
his face and not blinked an eye. The man was wrong
about Medron, too; Alaric remembered what the jester
had said about the court magician being a clever fake.
But that in no way lessened the very real danger that
the old man presented: *he* was convinced that he could
identify witches, and there was no way of knowing
what insignificant action might cause him to raise a
cry. More and more, Alaric wondered if he wasn't
wrong about seeking his fortune at Castle Royale. One
slip, like the reflexive self-defense of that day in Bedham Forest, would mean outlawry and perpetual pur-
suit. In eight months, he had not used his power once,
had steeled himself to forget it existed, but it glowed
deep within him still, as strong as ever. He balanced
the advantages: acceptance, companionship, physical
comfort, and infinite diversion in Castle Royale against

the nomadic existence of his childhood. There was no in-between. He was a minstrel, like it or not, and he had no desire to become a farmer or a man-at-arms for some small baron. He had to have a single rich patron or wander from village to village for a few coppers a year. Without a companion, the latter was no pleasant prospect. So he had to take his chances here, stifle the glow, and pretend to be a normal human being. He felt like a bird that had given up the lonely freedom of the skies for the security of a golden cage.

He turned his face away from the whispering pilgrims and drifted to sleep, and the delicate, pale face of Princess Solinde loomed in his dreams.

In the morning, he forced himself to greet the four pilgrims and break fast with them. He inquired after their destination as if he had not overheard their conversation the previous night.

"We go to the Holy Well at Canby," said the old man, "to drink and bathe and be cleansed."

"I wish you good speed on your journey," Alaric said.

"And good speed to yourself, minstrel, on your journey through life," replied the old man, his gnarled fingers drawing a fleeting holy sign in the air in front of Alaric's nose. "May you and your fine songs, that we heard yesterday, ever be safe from evil."

Alaric watched them troop out of the Great Hall in single file, the old man leading and the boy bringing up the rear. It seemed a good, though ironic, omen that a pilgrim as resolutely holy and evil-hating as the old man should denounce a false witch and bless a real one.

In midmorning, the King strode into the room—having broken fast in private—to judge civil and criminal

cases among the nobility. The jester ambled in behind
him, trailing a tiny wheeled cart containing variously
shaped trinkets. He planted himself at the King's knee
and sorted his colored baubles into two piles according
to some plan known only to himself. Occasionally, he
juggled three or four objects at once while His Majesty
deliberated. Alaric watched and listened for a time,
but finding the proceedings overlong, complex, and
tedious, he drifted away, his lute slung over his shoulder. His pack he left safe in the hands of the Palace
Oversteward. Navigating the twisting, branching corridor through which he had first entered the Palace
with ease, he returned to the side door that led to the
cobblestone courtyard. Outside, in the brilliant summer sunlight, his eyes were dazzled for a moment, and
when his vision cleared, he noted that a number of
men who had been practicing combat there the previous day were clustered about a pair of fighters in a
corner of the yard. One figure about his own size,
garbed in quilted gray cloth "armor" and steel helmet, tested his swordsmanship against a heftier man
in dirty blue. The two were slashing furiously with
wooden swords, and their wooden shields were splin-
tered and cracked. At last the smaller one heaved a
strong overhand blow at the heavier man's helm, striking the metal with a loud clunk, and that signaled the
end of the match.

"Well struck, my Lord Prince!" exclaimed the man
in blue, and he took off his helmet to reveal the ruddy,
sweating face and balding pate of a seasoned veteran.
"That would have split my head open!"

Prince Jeris removed his own helm and handed it
to the retainer who had stepped forward to receive
it. Dark hair was plastered in wet points across his
forehead, and he was breathing heavily, but he

grinned his satisfaction at his prowess and the compliment.

"Damn, it's hot, Falmar. I've got to get out of this suit!"

A second retainer stepped behind the young prince and deftly began to undo the complex lacings that held the quilted armor together. In a few moments, Jeris was able to shrug off the shirt and kick the leggings aside. Underneath, he wore only abbreviated breeches.

"Ho, it's the minstrel!" he exclaimed, spying Alaric in the throng. "Step aside and sing me a short song while I clear the dust from my throat." Jeris trotted to the scant shade of an overhanging roof, where a table of wines and cheeses was spread for his refreshment. He poured three cups of wine, handed one to his sparring partner, and indicated that the third was for Alaric.

"Thank you, Your Highness."

The prince tossed down his drink. "You can call me my Lord, minstrel. It feels less formal and far less cumbersome than spouting Your Highness in every sentence. The rest of you can go about your usual business." He waved at the crowd, which immediately dispersed, except for two unobtrusive armed guards who stood a few yards away. Jeris glanced sideways at Alaric. "Were you betting on me?"

"I wasn't aware that wagering was going on, my Lord."

"It was. Father doesn't allow it, but that won't stop them. They think it flatters me."

"And does it, my Lord?"

"Only Falmar's own praise flatters me." He poured himself a second cup of wine and sipped at it. "I see our jester has been thrown out of His Majesty's High

Court, as usual.'' He pointed past Alaric's left shoulder.

The minstrel turned and saw the dwarf skipping across the cobblestones toward them, his little wagon bouncing along behind. He chanted:

> *"Oh, blue is blue and red is red,*
> *But black and white are gray;*
> *The more you try to take yourself,*
> *The more you throw away!"*

He did a flip in midair and landed on his hands in front of the two young men. He peered at them upside down. "A bat may look at a prince," he sang.

Jeris laughed. "What have you done this time, motley?"

The jester lowered his legs, twisting as he did so, until he sat crosslegged on the warm cobblestones. "Baron Eglis . . ." His right hand plucked a blue cube from the pile of gewgaws in his wagon. ". . . who recently had that unfortunate accident which will forever deprive him of the ability to beget a legitimate heir, is suing the King . . ." His left hand chose a red ball. ". . . for permission to choose as his heir . . ." He transferred ball and cube to one hand and picked up a black pyramid with the other. ". . . his child by *droit du seigneur,* which he exercised for an entire week last year." He juggled the three playthings; the pyramid landed on top of his head, and the cube and ball each came to rest on one of his upturned palms. He winked at Jeris. "And so I was cast out of the High Court for presuming to anticipate the King's decision."

"Father ruled that the Barony would revert to the Crown when Eglis dies." The prince turned away, rubbing his cheek with the knuckles of his index finger. "Did you get the names of the child and its mother?"

The dwarf was arranging the contents of his wagon more neatly. "The mother is Dilia, quite a handsome wench, wife of a peasant named Marnit. The baby is Pon, now four months old."

Jeris nodded. "And where is my lovely sister?" he said in a lighter tone.

The jester stepped out of the shade and looked toward the sky speculatively, scanning it from horizon to horizon and up toward the zenith. "There," he said finally, pointing upward.

The prince leaned into the sunlight and glanced almost straight up, shading his eyes with one hand. He waved broadly toward the sky with the other.

Alaric followed the line of Jeris's gaze up the sheer masonry wall beside him, past two small windows to a third, set in the high tower just a few feet beneath its conical roof. Princess Solinde leaned from the opening, and her long dark tresses fluttered in the wind.

"Let down your hair!" shouted the jester.

"Foolish dwarf, she can't hear you. And I don't think she'll live long enough for her hair to grow *that* long."

"The lady approves of her brother's prowess with the wooden sword, or else she's letting the wind dry her hair. Who could tell from this distance?"

"Arm yourself, motley knave, and we'll give her a show with sharp-edged steel," Jeris said, leaning indolently against the wall.

The dwarf tapped the prince's right knee with two fingers. "Why, my Lord King would surely fire me if I caused his son to lose a leg. And where would I find another livelihood so plush?"

Jeris clapped the little man on the head and then

picked him up and swung him to a perch on his left shoulder. "The older I grow, the lighter you become, motley."

"And the higher becomes this seat of authority, Your Highness."

The prince boosted his small companion into the air, where the dwarf executed a series of rolls and landed on his feet on the ground.

"Come with me, my prince," the jester said, his eyes dancing and his cheeks red. "We will be traveling acrobats and earn our fortunes while seeing the world."

Jeris laughed. "Sometimes I think you're almost serious when you say that. Now, minstrel. . . ." He turned abruptly toward Alaric. "I haven't forgotten you standing here so silent. If you have some desire to hold a wooden sword, we can give my curious sister something to watch."

"I know nothing of swordsmanship, Your Highness."

"What, have you never wished to taste the reality of your songs?"

"I never had the opportunity. I am too poor to own a sword."

"What a fate! To sing forever of valorous deeds but never to *do* them. Motley, we must remedy this!"

"I will hold his lute," the jester offered.

"Wait, Your Highness! I'm not at all sure—"

"How did you manage to survive all this time without knowing anything of swordplay?"

"I've never had anything worth stealing, I avoid quarrels, and I run away if I must. I'm sure no one will ever write a song about me."

"Well, you might need it sometime, minstrel, and it's best learned early. Come on, we'll get some practical instruction from Falmar, and those wooden swords don't hurt nearly as much as one would think.''

In spite of his protests, Alaric soon found himself swaddled in quilting and paired off with a young squire who knew almost as little of the art of swordsmanship as Alaric did. They slashed awkwardly at each other, collected a few bruises, and gave up from exhaustion in a very short while. There was a certain exhilaration to even such a comparatively harmless exchange of blows—Alaric suddenly felt very masculine and self-assured, and these sensations stayed with him after he removed his quilted armor.

"You enjoyed it, didn't you, minstrel," said Jeris.

"Indeed, I did, my Lord."

"Practice well, and by spring you'll be able to face me. Ha! It'll be good to see a new nose beyond the other shield."

The midday meal found things much as they had been the previous day: the King sat at a low table on the dais, flanked by his children and the jester. But this day Alaric sat there, too, though at the far end away from the King, who signaled him to play while the others ate. Alaric himself dined afterward.

The princess wore scarlet today and a white kerchief covering her hair and veiling her forehead. Perhaps it was a trick of the light, but Alaric thought her eyes were red-rimmed and bloodshot, as if from weeping. She spoke little and only nodded to most of the conversational sallies aimed in her direction. She hardly touched her meal, passing most of it under the table to a pair of clamoring mastiffs. Her father finally noticed her behavior and remarked that she must be getting ill.

"I'm just not hungry, Father."

"Perhaps you need to be bled."

"No, thank you, Father. I'm all right."

Jeris leaned over and whispered something in her ear.

She shrugged, then nodded. "Father, may I be excused from the table?" When the King signaled with one hand, she rose and glided out of the room, her long skirts swishing softly.

"The Moon, you know, Father," Jeris said in an undertone.

"Ah, yes, the Moon. I hadn't thought of it."

"Perhaps some quiet music would soothe her. . . ."

"I know you want the minstrel as a playmate, my son." More loudly, he said, "Another song, Master Alaric, and then you may accompany the prince away."

A little later, the two young men passed through the familiar carved and gilded door. Inside the sitting room, Solinde reclined upon her velvet divan, her feet tucked under her crimson skirt, her head and back propped up by a dozen bolsters. In her hands was a black cloth that she was embroidering with fanciful flowers of red, purple, and blue. In a nearby chair, her maid Brynit embroidered in green on a small white glove.

"We've come to cheer you up, sister," Jeris said.

"Cheer me, then, with sad songs of love and death," she replied. She glanced up at Alaric, and when her gaze met his, her busy fingers fell suddenly still.

Alaric felt a flush of heat sweep through his body, and he yearned to cool himself in the bottomless oceans of her eyes. He dropped to one knee, lowering the lute to the rug beside him, and reached for her hands that lay like nestling birds in her lap. He touched her slim, white fingers, encircled them with his own, and drew them to his lips for a brief kiss.

"I will always sing anything you wish, my Lady Princess."

A firm hand touched his shoulder. Jeris. "If someone should chance to walk in, this would find our minstrel having a very short career in Castle Royale. Up, Master Alaric, and take a chair."

"Forgive me, Your Highness," Alaric murmured as he moved away from her.

"There is nothing to forgive," she said, and her fingers resumed their embroidery. "We will never speak of this, Brynit."

"Yes, ma'am," the maid replied, bobbing her head.

Safely ensconced in a high-backed chair, the young minstrel sang a song of love and heard the words of it for the first time. They fit her, moved toward her, seemed almost to be composed specifically for *her* hair, *her* eyes, *her* lips. As he sang, he reconsidered Dall's desire to come to Castle Royale someday. He tried to imagine Solinde as Dall had known her: a child of ten or so, not yet budded into womanhood, but promising charm and beauty with her every word, gesture, and expression. Was it only patronage that Dall had expected, or was it something more?

Later that day, the King sent for Alaric to play for two noblemen who arrived for an audience and a night's guesting. Still later, the youth slept restlessly by the fire in the Great Hall, and Dall's face haunted his dreams.

The days passed and the weeks passed. On alternate mornings, the minstrel would train with the squires, absorbing the skills of swordplay and horsemanship; at noon, he entertained the King's table; after sunset he would often be asked to play in the Great Hall until the torches guttered. Of the time that was his own, he devoted most to Jeris, who took him as a companion for hawking and deer and boar hunting, who taught him the game of draughts, and who secretly split a bottle of His Majesty's finest wine with him. The jester became a friend, too, and in spite of his initial refusal to teach the young man any sleight-of-hand tricks, he deftly demonstrated the palming of coins and other small objects, leaving Alaric to perfect the art on his own.

The only person in the Palace with whom he was not on friendly, or at least neutral, terms was Medron the wizard, that strange, silent, yet baleful figure who dined at a table of his own and only spoke to the King in a whisper inaudible to onlookers. He felt Medron's eyes on the back of his neck sometimes while singing in the Great Hall, and if he turned to test the accuracy of the feeling, he would see the man at his table or skulking in some dim corner. The wizard's eyes were black as pitch and sunk deep into his skull. He never smiled behind his beard but returned every glance with a cold stare. Did he see the *something* that the old pilgrim had spoken of?

The days passed and the weeks passed, and Medron, remaining silent, became part of the background blur of the Palace. Alaric found himself caught up in the routine of Palace life as if he had always been a part of it. He could almost fancy himself a nobleman, playmate of the prince and princess from their earliest years. But, of course, there was a line beyond which he dared not go, though often he found himself leaning over it.

One morning when he wasn't training in the courtyard, he sat in the high-backed chair in Solinde's sitting room while she wove on her loom, surrounded by her chattering maids. He sang a plaintive love song, oblivious to the whispers and titters of the girls, seeing only Solinde's flawless profile as she bent over the loom. He had a sudden urge to walk up behind her and kiss the tender nape of her neck, and he almost rose before a particularly loud giggle jarred him back to reality.

His fingers and lips remembered the softness of her hand, and he felt youth racing through his veins like fire. Three maids had already offered him liaisons, but pretty as they were, they faded to drabs beside Solinde. With every day that passed, her image swelled in his mind until it dominated him utterly. She drew his eye as a lodestone draws iron: whenever she entered a room, a thousand fantasy candles lighted; even though autumn waned, she kept summer in the Palace.

His own new attitude amazed him; previously he had always considered women a momentary diversion. His own songs of yearning and unrequited passion, which he sang so fervently—as Dall had taught him— had never meant anything to him. A woman he couldn't have had always been a woman he didn't want; another just like her waited somewhere beyond the next hill. Peasants or townspeople, they blurred together in his memory; dark-haired and fair, plump bodies and slim.

Somehow, in some way he couldn't recognize consciously, Princess Solinde was different.

She glanced up from her loom. "There is another verse, if I recall correctly."

Alaric strummed a discord. "The lover dies of longing. Too late his lady realizes that she cares for him and now can only strew roses on his grave. You see, Your Highness, why I prefer to leave it off."

"A sad fate, I suppose, if one assumes a person can die of longing."

"Well, if one forgets to eat. . . ."

Solinde laughed. "How like Dall you are! That is exactly what I would expect him to say!"

Then, as if her unintentional mention of the subject they had avoided discussing for many weeks jarred the good mood out of her, she bent intensely over her weaving once more. "You may go, minstrel. No doubt my father will soon be requiring your services."

The abrupt dismissal disappointed him—he had thought to remain as long as his voice held out—and he left dejectedly amid a flood of giggling farewells.

Downstairs, a cockfight was in progress, and the Great Hall was filled with shouts as the men crowded around the circle that had been cleared on the floor. The King himself presided and led the wagering. As the morning waned, the defeated roosters were thrown one by one into the pot for dinner. When all but the ultimate victor were dead, the King called on Alaric for some song appropriate to its triumph.

Evening fell at last, the torches were lit, and when his songs were no longer desired, Alaric went out into the courtyard. The air was brisk, and he drew his cloak tightly around his shoulders as he crossed the cobblestones. Above him, the stars shone clear and cold, and the tower which housed the princess's room rose to meet them. A pale yellow light flickered in the window, occasionally dimming as a passing body masked the flame. Alaric imagined it to be Solinde herself, clad only in a translucent nightgown—though in this weather it would more likely be flannel—and he wondered if she would come to the window. How many nights had he stood here like a character from one of his songs, hoping for one last glimpse of her before he slept?

To his right, from a parapet overlooking the yard, came the metallic sounds of the mailed night guard making his rounds. They ceased as the man leaned into an embrasure to survey the yard.

"Who is there?" he demanded of the dark-cloaked minstrel.

Alaric strummed his lute in reply, improvising a verse about the long, tedious hours of night guard duty, and the watchman walked on.

With a last glance upward, the youth sighed, shivered, and retraced the tortuous route that led to his sleeping place. Halfway there, he was met by Brynit, the princess's plump little maid, who carried a lit candle stub whose wavering flame she shielded with one cupped palm.

"My Lady's not feeling well this night and wishes a few songs to while away the darkness, minstrel," she said.

Alaric bowed elaborately to conceal his excitement. "If Her Highness wishes, I will sing till the birds begin." He offered the maid his arm, but she turned on her heel and led the way.

The Great Hall had settled down while the minstrel was outside, and only the whispers of the pages assigned to stoke the hearths could be heard above sporadic snores and sleepy mutters. Brynit climbed the stairs quietly, lifting the front of her dress well above her knees; Alaric followed, trying not to tread on her short train. At the top of the stairs, in the puddle of light shed by the wall-torch, the guard reclined. One of his knees was bent, the other straight out before him. His spear rested across his lap, and his head lolled forward, bobbing occasionally as he breathed heavily.

"Is he all right?" Alaric whispered, stooping to look at the man's face.

Brynit touched the minstrel's arm and motioned him onward peremptorily. She stepped over the unconscious guard.

Smelling nothing but strong wine, Alaric straightened and gingerly passed the man. He glanced back once before they reached the door of the carved birds, and the scene had not changed.

Inside, the sitting room was transformed by dimness to a tapestry-lined cave. No one was there. Alaric walked toward the chair he usually occupied and started to place his lute upon the seat.

"This way," said Brynit. She stood by the far wall, one plump arm holding aside a hanging to reveal another door. It opened.

The other room was the one with the window, the princess's bedchamber. It was small and cosy, three walls hung with woolen panels and the fourth, opposite the window, occupied by a fireplace containing a roaring fire that warmed the room considerably more than two hearths warmed the Great Hall. In the center of the chamber, resting on a round brown rug, stood the princess's bed.

"Good evening, minstrel," said Solinde. She reposed on a cushioned boudoir chair near the fire.

"Is there something else, Your Highness?" asked the maid.

Solinde shook her head.

Brynit curtseyed low and left the room, closing the door behind herself.

"Won't you sit down?" said the princess.

Alaric glanced around. The only other chair was beside the bed, close to the window. He sat there and shrugged off his cloak. The room was pleasantly warm even though the window shutters were slightly ajar to allow in fresh air.

The princess stood up and walked around the bed toward him, passing in front of the fire as she did so. Her pale blue gown became translucent for a moment, exposing her youthful contours to Alaric's eye, and as he stopped breathing he could hear his pulse hammering wildly at his temples. He forced his gaze upward to her face, framed by unbound dark hair over which the flames laced red highlights.

"Am I pretty?" she asked.

"Yes, Your Highness. More than pretty."

She stepped nearer and touched his shoulder with her left hand. "Would you like to kiss me?"

His hand crept up of its own accord and covered her fingers. "What will happen if someone should come here now?" he whispered.

"No one moves at this time of night, not even Father. You saw the guard—he'll wake before dawn and merely think the night unusually short. And Brynit, who has served me faithfully most of my life, is watching the corridor."

"What do you want of me, Your Highness?"

"Nothing. Everything." Her hand moved up his shoulder to the back of his neck, and she was closer, much closer, her body brushing the arm of his chair. "You have no idea of what it's like to be a princess. Everyone very polite, very afraid to offend. No one dares touch me but Father and Jeris and the maids. Yet I've been a woman for four years now, and I want to be touched." Her hand moved over Alaric's close-cropped hair. "*One* would not have been afraid, but he came too early . . . would you like to kiss me, minstrel?" She knelt on the floor beside his chair, and her hand slipped down his arm and came to rest on his knee.

"I've wanted to kiss you for a long time, my princess." He held her face between his palms and bent forward to press a chaste kiss against her forehead. He breathed in the scent of her hair and felt dizzy. Her cheeks were hot beneath his hands, or perhaps it was his own skin that blazed. He kissed the tip of her nose, and then he saw her lips, upturned, waiting for him like a blossom awaits a butterfly. He tasted them for a long moment—they were cool and soft—and his hands moved back, tangling in her hair.

"Again," she said.

"I can't trust myself again, Your Highness." He forced his hands to let go of her, to push her away gently. He rose, reaching for his cloak and lute.

She clasped him, clinging, staying him with the pressure of breast and hip and thigh. Her arms locked about his waist, and as she tossed her head her hair trapped his upper body in a silken net. "Don't leave me," she whispered.

Their lips met hungrily now, and their tongues fenced. His hands grew bold, caressing her body through the single thin layer of cloth. He bent her back till they lay prone on the bed, and she never pulled away but urged him closer. Soon her gown was twisted around her waist and he could stroke her naked flesh while she found the lacings of his tunic and breeches.

"Oh, be gentle, my love, I'm a virgin," she whispered, but her body had no fear of violence as it squirmed and thrashed beneath him. For an instant, he felt a slight resistance at the juncture of her thighs, but one abrupt motion allowed him to pierce her maidenhead.

"I love you, Solinde," he whispered as they rocked to and fro.

Then a sound penetrated the haze of his pleasure:

voices. Footsteps. The thud of a door swung all the way back on its hinges. He froze, all desire suddenly draining away from his body. He thrust Solinde away from him, rolled across the bed, dived for his cloak and lute . . .

. . . and hit the cold cobblestones hard, bruising his right shoulder. The lute twanged softly as it bumped the ground beside him; he felt it all over till he was sure it was undamaged and until his eyes became accustomed to outdoor blackness. He laced up his awry clothing and wrapped the cloak tightly about his quivering shoulders. Sweat dripping down his neck chilled him, and he wiped it away with the back of one hand. When his eyes were dark-adapted, he looked at the parapet—the guard was out of sight for a moment.

Alaric stood and nearly fell over again. A strip of the princess's sheet was tangled about his ankles—in his haste to escape, he'd taken it with him. He wadded the fabric up and stuffed it into the hole of his lute.

High above his head, the shutters of Solinde's window were flung wide, and the light within flickered wildly as people passed back and forth behind the casement.

Staring upward, he felt dead inside. It was all over. Right at this moment, she was probably confessing everything to her father, if she wasn't in hysterics from his damned show of instinctive self-preservation. Tears brimmed in his eyes for the first time in many weeks; he didn't want to leave and he dared not stay. A single instant would suffice to whisk him to the Forest of Bedham where he could sit by Dall's lonely grave and meditate upon the lovely woman that neither of them could have. But he delayed, looking up toward her window, hoping against hope that she would lean out to let her hair float on the wind, that he might see her one more time.

The shutters closed.

"Still awake, minstrel?" called the night guard.

"Just going in," Alaric replied, and he stepped quickly into the shelter of the doorway, fearing unreasonably that the man was readying his spear. He pressed against the chill stone wall, telling himself over and over that the word could not have spread so quickly.

And still he stayed, tracing the familiar route to the Great Hall. He had a vague desire to get his knapsack from the Oversteward, to be warm again for a little while, to see familiar faces before he bid them farewell forever. Just as he entered the hall, the King passed through, swiftly and suddenly, clad in his nightwear and a crimson cloak; anger showed on his face, but as he neared Alaric, who was one of the few awake and standing, he nodded a greeting and strode on. The jester trailed after him, and in sudden desperation, Alaric drew the little man aside.

"What's going on? Why is the King abroad so late?"

The dwarf shrugged, grinding sleep out of his eyes with the heel of one hand. "Rumor went out that the Lady Solinde was abed with a man, but when the King's righteous wrath went to investigate, the princess was found abed with herself and no other, peacefully asleep and loath to wake. As who wouldn't be at this ridiculous hour? A certain informant may be finding herself a new job in the laundry before long. Good night, minstrel, before the birds awaken."

Alaric stepped back into the shadows of his usual sleeping place as the royal entourage disappeared from view. His mind was juggling the idea of safety, afraid to accept it, afraid that all that had transpired since he left Solinde was a dream taking place in the split second before he appeared in the courtyard. He pinched his arm, and the pain seemed real. He stamped his foot, and the muttered grumblings of sleepers sounded real.

He had to talk to Solinde. He had to explain himself, defend himself, assure himself that she was as calm and unafraid as the dwarf's words implied. But there was no way; surely a maid would be sleeping in her room now—he dared not take a chance on being discovered now that he seemed to be safe.

He found a stray quilt and curled up into a troubled sleep. In his dreams, Solinde alternately screamed and kissed him.

Outside, dawn was barely breaking over the courtyard, but in the depths of Castle Royale, eternal night ruled. Flickering torches cast wild shadows against the walls, and low moans floated in the air like wisps of smoke. Brynit, the princess's faithful retainer, made her cautious way to the underground alchemical hideaway of Medron the magician. The stone stairs leading downward were slippery with dampness and fungi, and as her fingers trailed the walls for balance, they picked up a slimy coating. At every step, she held her breath and listened, but the loudest sound she heard was the terror-filled beating of her own heart.

At last she reached the massive oaken door to Medron's chamber. A heavy knocker hung at eye level. She grasped it, pulled outward, and allowed it to descend with a muffled clang. Long moments passed, and the door swung slowly inward, revealing Medron himself, swathed in a gray robe spattered with stains of all shapes and colors.

"What do you want?" he said.

Brynit curtseyed nervously. "I need a charm, Lord Medron. A powerful charm against a witch."

He eyed her fiercely. "Come in." He stepped aside to let her enter.

Within was a warm, comparatively dry room of long tables and strangely shaped vessels of ceramic and glass containing colored liquids both cloudy and clear. On the far side of the chamber was a large fireplace that connected somewhere above with one of the hearths in the Great Hall, through which, occasionally, foul smells emanated. A bright blaze filled the fireplace. Overhead, in the corners of the room, were grates through which fresh, cold air entered.

Medron seated himself on one of a pair of stools near the hearth and motioned for Brynit to take the mate. "You must tell me who this witch is and why you fear her."

"*Him*," said Brynit. "Alaric the minstrel. He's bewitched my Lady to love him, and this night she arranged to have him visit her bedchamber after His Majesty slept."

Medron shrugged, "This is nothing but the way of young people."

Brynit twisted her handkerchief unmercifully. "So I thought. I've been my Lady's maid almost since she was born, and she's like a sister to me, or even a daughter. I saw this young man and saw her eye on him, and I thought, well, he's well enough made . . . but his Majesty would have my head if I allowed such fancies to go on. The boy is common and low and hardly a fit lover for my Lady. She wheedled and begged and ordered until at last I told her I would help; we gave the stairway guard a sleeping draught my Lady once had for her vapors. The boy came upstairs, and I left them alone together."

Medron plucked at his beard. "And so?"

She squirmed atop the stool and kicked her legs like a bashful child.

"There's a chink in the wall between sitting room and bedchamber . . . I've arranged the hangings so that I can see the one from the other. When I was sure that . . . I locked the door and called His Majesty immediately, then returned to watch again." The handkerchief was wound tightly around her white-knuckled fingers by this time. "As the King entered the sitting room, making a great deal of noise, I saw the boy . . . I saw the boy fly out the window!"

Medron stood suddenly. "What?"

"Yes, yes, he flew out the window and my Lady fainted."

The magician began to pace back and forth before the fireplace. "Now, this is a serious charge you bring. Can you recall *exactly* what happened?"

"Oh, yes, *exactly!* The minstrel flew past his cloak and lute, which were lying in the chair beside the bed, grabbed them and went on out the window. When we entered the bedchamber, he was gone. The King never saw him and of course assumed no one had been there. I didn't dare tell, my Lord Medron, until I got a charm from you. I'm so frightened . . . he'll turn me into a toad if I tell without a charm, won't he?"

"He might." Medron went to the nearest table and stood beside it, tapping his fingers on the smooth surface. "How long ago did this happen?"

"*This very night!* The King has threatened to send me to the laundry for lying, my Lord. Please help me!" She slipped off the stool and fell to her knees before the magician. "I will give you whatever I have.

What could I need as a toad? Anything you wish, my Lord!''

Medron looked down at the short, plump, plain woman cringing before him. "Not for you will I do this, silly wench, but for *her.* Come, I will make you a charm to wear about your neck, and you will be able to sleep. In the morning we will bring this matter before the King.''

The next morning passed as many mornings had for Alaric: in mock combat. He did badly, being vanquished more often than usual. He was nervous, and his strokes were wilder than normal, but when the exercise was finished, he felt less tense.

Jeris commented as they were sipping wine in the shade of the overhanging roof. "Did last night's uproar rouse you, too? I thought I'd never get back to sleep.''

Alaric nodded.

The prince chuckled. "Father was rather annoyed at being awakened for nothing.''

A clattering on the far side of the courtyard, accompanied by a great outburst of mutters from bystanders, caused the two young men to look in that direction. The magician Medron, flanked by four mailed guards with halberds, approached. His long black robe, embroidered in red and yellow with astrological symbols, swept the cobblestones, raising a cloud of dust. In his outstretched hands he held a short rope twisted of white satin and silver cord. He stopped in front of Alaric and Jeris and made a few passes in the air with the rope while he murmured unintelligibly under his breath. Then he deftly looped a slip knot around the minstrel's left wrist and pulled it tight.

"Alaric the minstrel," he intoned, "in the name of

all that is holy, I bind you over to the judgment of the High Court on the charge of witchcraft!''

''What's this?'' said Jeris.

Alaric was paralyzed and could only stare at his trapped wrist. The cord meant nothing, of course; he could disappear and take it with him if he chose, or with a little more concentration, leave it hanging limply from Medron's fingers. It was a symbol, though, of the resumption of the wanderer's life which he had wanted so much to leave behind and which he had thought, for a night, he was free of.

''You will accompany me,'' said the magician.

Alaric glanced at Jeris and shrugged.

''I forbid this!'' said the prince. ''State the reasons for your vile accusation!''

''I will do so in the King's court, and you will do well to hold your tongue while the King's commands are carried out.''

Jeris's face reddened, but he fell behind and allowed the magician and the guards to lead Alaric indoors.

Alaric bent to retrieve his lute from the corner in which it rested, but one of the guards snatched it from beneath his fingers and carried it along. Again, the youth shrugged. He thought bleakly of the future; he would wait to see her once more and then he would vanish in front of the entire court, perhaps taking a section of the floor with him as a parting gesture. He thought longingly of lifting Solinde in his arms and taking *her* along to live in some foreign land, but he knew that was impossible—she would be too well guarded, too well surrounded. Even using his power to get close . . . before he could swing her free of the floor to be sure of taking her whole body along, he would be impaled by a dozen spears. No, alone he would go, and he would have to make this last memory of her worth a lifetime of running from the King.

"And what do you have to say for yourself, witch?" the King shouted as soon as Alaric entered the Great Hall.

"Only that it is not true," the minstrel replied softly when he reached the foot of the throne and bowed.

"Let the first witness be called!"

The guard who had slept at the top of the stairs stepped forward and knelt to the King. "I saw no one pass, Your Majesty. If he entered the princess's room, he must have been invisible."

"Let the second witness be called."

The night guard who walked the parapet presented himself. "I saw the minstrel in the courtyard after everyone was asleep. He was not there for the space of five rounds, then I heard his lute again and saw a shadowy figure. I called out and his voice answered, and then I saw him go inside."

"Let the third witness be called!"

Brynit stepped forward. She wore a gaudy red and yellow amulet about her neck. "He burst in on us as the princess readied for bed, Your Majesty. I found myself bewitched, moving backward into the sitting room. Then, the bedchamber door, of its own accord, closed and locked." She pulled herself up to her full height of four and a half feet and glared at Alaric defiantly. "I called out to the downstairs guard to rouse His Majesty, our own guard being in some sort of bewitched stupor, and while they dallied I pounded on the door, which did not yield. At last, I remembered a spy-hole which was used when political prisoners were kept in the tower, and I looked into the princess's bedchamber. My Lady was helpless, and the witch was working his will on her poor limp body. I screamed and called on the Holy Name, but none of it affected this powerful witch. Then, as Your Majesty arrived," she fingered her amulet, "I saw the witch grab his lute and his cloak and fly out the open window, banging it shut behind him!"

"Oh, Father, this is monstrous!" screamed Solinde as she tore away from the arms of a number of ladies who had held her in an obscure corner behind the throne. She ran across the dais and down the steps, her dark hair flying behind her, her cheeks flaming angrily, until the King caught the sleeve of her blue dress and swung her around. "He is no witch!" she cried.

"Neither are you a virgin," the King replied. "If not last night, when?"

She looked away and her eyes caught Alaric's, scant yards away. "Oh, why have you stayed?" she murmured.

"Hush, child," said the King, jerking her arm sharply. "Your bewitched mind is clouded with false love of this fiend." In a kindlier tone: "Lord Medron shall cure you, my daughter, just as successfully as he has caught and bound this witch." He handed her over to a lady-in-waiting who had come hurrying up. "Now, witch, that tower is sheer; the only way to enter it other than the stairs is by flight, and our faithful Brynit has confessed to *seeing* you fly. Therefore, what say you?"

Alaric still looked at Solinde, etching his vision of her loveliness indelibly on his brain. "I say that the faithful Brynit is a liar. I can no more fly that you can."

"The evidence is against you, witch. Have you a final request before I pass sentence?"

For an instant Alaric felt more like laughing than anything else. If a band of roving actors had presented this situation as a farce, Alaric would have helped to boo them off the stage. He sighed. "May I have my lute?"

Medron stepped forward, still holding one end of the white and silver cord attached to Alaric's wrist. "I am most interested in this lute," he said. "The maid has attested that he took the lute as he flew out the window. Might I examine the instrument?"

The King nodded, and Medron slipped the end of the cord into his belt to free both hands to receive the lute. He turned it over, shook it curiously, and then his skinny fingers deftly reached between the strings and plucked white fabric from the hole. He held the wrinkled cloth out for all to see.

"A corner ripped out of my Lady's sheet!" exclaimed Brynit. "It was missing this morning when I straightened the bed!"

"I think we may assume," said Medron, holding the rag gingerly between his two fingers, "that this is the object through which he controls the princess, with the aid of the lute. As part of her cure, I will burn them both."

"And we will do the same for her bewitcher," announced the King, rising to his feet.

Regretting the loss of his lute and riveting his eyes on Solinde, Alaric chose between a number of places he was able to travel to. Yet he hesitated, just to see her face for another moment, and another, and another.

The jester cartwheeled past him and up onto the dais.

"Away, motley," said the King. "We're to burn a witch today." He stepped past the little man, descended from the dais and stood before Alaric, towering over him. "I am not afraid of you, witch." And he slapped the young man across the mouth.

Alaric fell to his knees, his head spinning and his

ears ringing. For a moment, the hot anger that rose in his chest tempted him to take the King's leg with him as he disappeared, leaving only a bloody stump. Or even to spring for the monarch's head and leave a corpse behind. Revulsion for the very thought made him gag, and as his brain cleared, he knew he couldn't do any of it. He had to be satisfied by noting, from the corner of his eye, that Medron, too, had been thrown off balance by the slap, had lost the end of the white and silver cord, and had to scrabble for it frantically.

"If you're going to burn a witch, you'll have to look farther than this room for one," piped the dwarf.

"Quiet, motley," replied the King. "On your feet, witch, and march to your pyre!"

"Your Majesty, I have something here that will certainly interest your pious soul."

The King turned reluctantly. "What is it? Quickly!"

"The device by which our poor minstrel escaped Her Highness's room without relying on the power of flight." The small metal object he handed the King was a long spike with the blunt end bent into a ring. "It was hammered into the wall outside Her Highness's window. A rope twice long enough to reach from courtyard to window is coiled inside the quilt the minstrel slept in last night. Two guards were with me when these items were found and will gladly vouch for the truth of my statements. Can the faithful maid Brynit say as much?" He turned toward the short, plump woman expectantly.

Brynit shrank back, fingering her amulet and looking at Medron. "It was not bright in the room, but still I know what I saw. . . ."

"And she saw him diving through the window escape by the rope, nothing more," said the d

"He took the lute in order to leave no evidence, and the fragment of sheet is easily explained under the energetic circumstances." The jester cleared his throat noisily and winked at Alaric.

"She lied about everything," Solinde said in a cold voice. "I begged her to help me meet him alone, and she agreed. We mixed a sleeping potion for the guard, and *that* is why he saw nothing. *She* fetched him and *she* let him into my room, and then she betrayed me. I swear on my mother's grave that all this is true. I spit on you, Brynit. Father, if this woman remains my maid, I will kill her."

The King stepped back and glanced from his daughter to Alaric, who was just climbing unsteadily to his feet. "This becomes another matter entirely."

"Father, I love this man."

"You are young. This love will pass and leave you ready to make a proper marriage."

"I will always love him." She tried to step forward, but the ladies held her back.

"Alaric the minstrel, this is my decision: we will do without your songs from this time forward. I give you a horse and one week to reach the border. After that, you are a dead man in my realm. Go." He whispered to a nearby guard, then strode out of the room.

Alaric dusted himself off and shucked the white and silver rope with a show of distaste. He snatched his lute from Medron, who merely sniffed superciliously and walked away. The hall emptied quickly; Solinde was dragged away even as she gazed sadly back at him ⸺er one shoulder. At length, he was left alone with ⸺jester and the guard to whom the King had whis-⸺d.

⸺m to give you Lightfoot," said the guard.

⸺no doubt to kill him as soon as we enter the

stable," commented the dwarf. "You may walk ahead. We will follow at considerable distance."

The guard led the way.

"Well, this is good-by, motley."

"Let's stop with the Oversteward and pick up your knapsack."

They did that.

"I wish I could say good-by to Solinde."

"Perhaps she'll wave from the tower."

But when he looked up toward her room, the window was shuttered.

"I wish. . . ."

"That you could undo it all?" supplied the dwarf.

"I don't know. I love her."

"You'll sing your songs much better after this."

"Does it go away—this empty feeling?"

"I don't know."

"Have you ever loved, motley?"

"A few times. A man like me can't really take things like that too seriously."

Alaric glanced at him in surprise and saw a big-headed, funny looking dwarf and knew he wasn't alone in his despair.

Leading the gray horse, they crossed the drawbridge and stepped onto the dirt road that had brought the minstrel to the castle so many weeks before. It had been deep summer then, but now the wind was chill and winter was near. Dry leaves swirled against their legs.

A clatter of hoofs caused Alaric to glance back once more. It was Jeris, astride a coal-black war-horse divested of its heraldic trappings.

"I'll ride a little way with you," he said.

At the dwarf's suggestion, Alaric lifted him up to a perch behind Jeris, and then he mounted his own, smaller nag. In silent companionship, they ambled along the road until the forest closed in and hid the castle from sight, forcing Alaric to stop looking back every few seconds.

"This is as far as I can go," said Jeris when they reached a bend in the road.

Alaric looked up at the prince, who towered over him much as the King had. He caught the youth's gloved left hand and bowed his head over it. "I'm sorry, my Lord."

Jeris clapped him on the shoulder. "She needed it. And more. We'll miss you, minstrel. She'll plague me with you for a long time, I know. Here, she gave me this for you." From the pouch at his waist he drew a square of black cloth embroidered with fanciful flowers of red, purple, and blue.

"I remember it well. It was for Dall, but now I'm gone, too." He folded it carefully and tucked it inside his lute. "This makes a better favor than a bit of sheeting."

"And from me, I thought you'd find this useful." From the bag on the left side of his saddle, Jeris drew a belt and a sword in tooled-leather scabbard. "At worst, you can sell it for a reasonable sum." He handed it over.

"And from me," said the dwarf, "this." In his open palm lay the spike that had changed Alaric's fate. "I knew it would be useful someday."

The minstrel drew a deep breath. "You know."

"We know," said Jeris. "Solinde thought your life in danger and confided in us. But I think her fears were groundless—they could never burn you. Am I right?"

Alaric nodded.

"Still, existence as a known witch would be unpleasant. As things are, you trail the glory of having seduced a princess, a reputation which will certainly have its advantages." He clasped Alaric's hand. "I want to say that when I am King you'll be welcome here again . . . but Father will probably live a long, long while, and by the time you could return there would be nothing but me and motley to return for. Good luck, my friend, and take care of yourself." He wheeled his horse and galloped away while the jester hung on with one hand and waved with the other.

Alaric pulled his cloak more tightly around his shoulders. A bitter wind was rising.

Inn of the
Black Swan

THE YOUNG MINSTREL WAS TIRED AND HUNGRY, and he wished mightily that, like his steed, he could derive nourishment from the limp brownish grass exposed by melting snowdrifts at the edge of the road. He let the animal veer left or right as it pleased, to crop the meager growth. Formerly, Lightfoot had been well-fed, cared for in royal stables; he had even worn gaudy heraldic trappings on a few appropriate holidays. Now, his ribs showed, his neck drooped, his mane and tail hung matted with neglect.

Alaric's worn knapsack, which dangled from the pommel of his saddle, contained an extra shirt and three lute strings, but not a scrap of bread. He had ridden since sunrise on an empty belly, hoping to find a patron, no matter how low in station, who would be willing to trade a meal for an evening's entertainment. In three long days, he had passed no cultivated land, nor any sign but the meandering road itself that civilization had ever traveled this way. He was tempted, sorely tempted, to turn back lest he fall off the edge of the world, which this near-impenetrable forest would surely hide until the final, fatal moment. Yet the road existed, its earth trampled flat by countless hooves and feet; it must lead somewhere. To Durman, a small kingdom on the banks of a vast river—so said the head of a great house on the fringes of the forest, but his tone was uncertain, as if the place were merely legendary. Still, Alaric pressed on, for there was nothing behind to keep him.

A white rabbit, its fur blending so well with a patch of snow that Alaric had glanced directly at the creature without seeing it, bounded into the air as Lightfoot's hoof passed near. The minstrel plucked his dagger from its sheath, tossed it with the determination of hunger, and missed as the cottontail scrambled for the sheltering shadows of the trees. Alaric dismounted and retrieved the knife with a grimace, regretting for the hundredth time that he was such a poor hunter. Dall had always downed a bird or deer on the rare occasions when the minstrel pair could find no work in large house or small or in some village square. His had been the hawk's eye and the sure hand; the bow was buried with him—Alaric, whose arm never improved, had no use for it.

As a furtive, half-feral child, he had stolen his food and other things as well: clothing, money, trinkets that he would hoard, squirrellike in his bower in the woods. Dall had broken him of the habit and shown him how to earn his living honestly. Minstrelsy had turned from labor to pleasure during the years they spent together, but Alaric had never forgotten how to steal.

He tethered his horse near a particularly large clump of grass and removed the heavy saddle. He doffed his cloak and the lute he wore beneath it, gently wrapping the instrument against the chill air and laying it across the saddle, so that only the tip of its sharply angled neck touched the damp ground. Then he backed off till he was out of sight—Lightfoot, having been trained for combat, did not shy easily, but his master preferred to take no chances. He stepped behind a tree and disappeared.

For an instant, the hen house was silent, then all bedlam broke out as the startled birds scattered in every direction, flapping their wings and squawking in terror, bouncing off walls and perches and Alaric's body, clawing each other and shedding clouds of feathers. Alaric grabbed a small one and vanished.

In the depths of the forest once more, he wrung the creature's neck and began the tedious task of plucking it. This was the second bird he had stolen from that hen house—the only hen house he knew well enough to travel to in his own peculiar manner—and he felt vaguely guilty about doing so. The peasant to whom it belonged owned more fowl than he could, perhaps, count, but he had been a kindly man, not the sort Alaric preferred to steal from. Some weeks earlier, he and his family had guested the minstrel for two days and nights, exchanging their wholesome food and a clean straw bed for entertainment and a bit of help with their chores. Gathering eggs and sweeping up the litter of droppings and feathers had given Alaric an excellent opportunity to memorize the contours and location of the hen house.

Memory had served him well in the forest, else he would have gone hungry. But he knew that the theft must not continue. Eventually, the peasant would notice that he had too few chickens; perhaps he would assume that a quick-witted fox, emboldened by the isolation of the farm was raiding the coop. He would set traps, he might even mount a guard, and ultimately he would discover that the marauder was a witch who was just as vulnerable to injury and death as any predator, though a bit more agile than even the lithest cat. Alaric had no desire to pit his agility against the skill and speed of a bowman.

He thought again of giving up the trek, of turning back to regions better known, where he could sing to fill his clamorous belly. But something drew him west: the stars, the setting sun, his own curiosity, or the vagrant whim of his horse. Something made him roam with a restless yearning, and what it was that he yearned for, beyond the woman left far behind, he could not guess.

Roasted on a spit, the plump chicken was succulent and delicious. By the time Alaric had buried the well-picked bones and gathered a store of wood sufficient for the night, the gloom of the forest had deepened till the boughs overhanging the road were merely vast dark masses among which an occasional star glinted. He pushed the fire aside with a large forked branch, added some kindling to keep it alight in its new location, and settled himself on the bare spot it had warmed. Wrapped in his cloak and blanket, his battered cap pulled low to shield his hair from the splashing off-spring of thawing icicles high above, he plucked a plaintive melody from his lute. Apart from his own music and the endless dripping that formed steep-sided, finger-wide holes in the moist snow of winter's end, the forest was silent; even the wind, which often blew gustily at this time of year, could not penetrate the multitudinous trees.

He sang a song of wandering, one he had often sung during this season—so often that his voice no longer required his brain to remind it of the words. His thoughts rambled, cued by a phrase here and there, to his footloose, aimless childhood, to Dall, and to Castle Royale and Solinde. He was thinking of her before he realized it, remembering too well the last time they had been together, in her father's court. He could see her grieving eyes, hear her futile declaration of love. As so often before, he fought the impulse to return— he knew every step of the way, he could be there in a heartbeat, he could see her face and kiss her sweet lips.

His fingers tightened on the lute. Inside was Solinde's keepsake, her kerchief, embroidered with her own hands in honor of Dall but given for remembrance to *him*. Her farewell gift. Alaric had no doubt that a maid or two slept in the princess's chamber every night now, to make certain no eager young man crept into her bed. Nor was she alone in daylight; even in the old days, a maid or a flock of giggling playmates had followed her almost everywhere during waking hours. To chance that she might be accompanied by no one but her brother or the dwarf was to chance branding her with the stigma of having loved a witch.

Or of bearing a witch's child. It was unlikely, he knew, but not impossible.

He recalled his own foster mother who, though she had not borne him herself, had nevertheless earned the fear and suspicion of her neighbors by taking him into her hut. Thereafter, people began to come to her for charms and potions, though she always insisted she knew nothing of magic. She was fortunate—he learned when he was much older—that no cows sickened and died mysteriously while she was raising her foster son.

What would the King, that witch-burner of great renown, do if his own daughter bore a witch's babe? Kill the child, of course, but also kill *her*, the fruit of his own body? Or would he trust his faithful magician to cure her of the enchantment and ever after wonder how effective the cure had been?

No, it was best not to take the chance of being caught, best for Alaric and best for Solinde. He told himself so over and over, especially late at night, when his desire for her was most intense. He had thought that a few months would heal the raw wound of exile—he had never cared, before, where he stayed or where he went—but it had not; the wound was deeper than that. He knew with dread certainty that someday it would drive him back to her. Someday he would kneel at her feet and beg her to fly with him. He, a wandering minstrel with no possessions but the clothing on his back and a mangy horse that had once belonged to her father. What kind of life could he offer a woman accustomed to servants, vast chambers lined with tapestries, furs, satins, and jewels? None. She would be a fool to accept. And he feared that of the two of them, she was not the fool. Perhaps, distracted by the diversions of court life, she had already forgotten him.

One more night passed in which he stayed away from Castle Royale.

Late the next afternoon, he came upon a clearing on the left side of the road; poking out of the drifted snow were naked stalks that had once, not so many months before, been heavy with grain. Wondering if the planter still lived nearby, Alaric shouted and whistled, rising in his stirrups to scan the field. Movement caught his eye: a head cautiously raised above the bent and broken stubble.

"Hello," Alaric said in a pleasant tone. He smiled and spread his arms wide to show that he held no weapon. "Can you tell me how much farther the forest continues toward the west?"

The head rose higher; it belonged to a thickset man of middle age. He walked forward, slapping aside with one arm the wet stalks that blocked his way. He was dressed in drab brownish homespun, and he carried a scythe on his shoulder. "Not much farther. Who would you be?"

"Alaric is my name, a poor minstrel looking for honest work and a meal."

"I see a scabbard peeking out behind you. Is there a sword inside?"

"There is, but I'm no bandit, rest assured. Can you spare a crust, good farmer, or a bowl of gruel?"

"There are rabbits in the woods."

Alaric sighed and slid off his horse. "I am no hunter, I fear. Since my knapsack emptied, I've been hungry, and poor Lightfoot has seen too little grass for his liking."

"I have no food to spare, but there is an inn a half-day's journey westward, where the road passes near the river."

"Good sir, the sun will soon set, and my mount and I are tired and hungry. In the name of common humanity, let me work for our meals and sleep warm this night, even if it must be with your cows and sheep."

The peasant considered this for a long time, looking Alaric up and down as if to see some sign of good or bad will upon his body. He frowned mightily and stroked the blade of his scythe, but at last he said, "Perhaps you are too young to be dishonest. Come along this way." Instead of leading, he motioned for Alaric to cross the field of stubble ahead of him.

Lightfoot made one attempt to crop the straw, but Alaric urged him onward and, either because he was well-trained or because the straw was exceptionally poor fodder, he obeyed.

Beyond the field, enough forest land had been cleared to accommodate a small group of buildings. Nearest the road was the sturdy, windowless wooden barn; a fence attached to it formed an enclosure for three cows, a calf, and a bull. Next was the hen house, from which emanated not only the cackle and flutter of chickens but also the dreamy cooing of doves. Far-

ther on stood the stone and plank cabin which served
the peasant as living quarters; its tall chimney spewed
a comforting volume of dark smoke.

The man rapped loudly on the cabin door, and in a
few moments it opened a crack, revealing a dim interior and a bright eye set in a fair-skinned face.

"An extra bowl of supper," said the peasant, jerking a thumb toward Alaric.

The eye bobbed to indicate comprehension, and the
door slammed shut.

"Now, if you are really willing to work for your
supper, follow me."

They put Lightfoot in the barn with a pile of hay,
and the peasant selected an axe from the rack of farm-
ing implements in the rear of the building. At the edge
of the clearing, where trees stripped of their lower
branches showed that firewood had been gathered
there, he handed Alaric the axe and bade him chop.
Then he stood back, too far away for easy conversation, and pretended to be busy with his scythe and
something close to the ground. Actually, he did nothing but watch the minstrel, clearly uneasy about an
edged weapon in unpredictable hands. He only called
a halt and claimed the axe when the last rays of the
sun were about to fade behind the forest.

Alaric stumbled to the already sizable woodpile
with the fruits of his labor, barely able to stack it in
some semblance of order. His arms felt as if they
were about to drop off, and his back was a pillar of
fire; he hadn't had so much exercise since the days
of his battle-training in the courtyard of Castle Royale.

For supper, he was not allowed inside the house;
instead, a bowl of gray porridge and a chunk of brown
bread were passed through the partially open door. He
saw a little more of that blue eye and fair face this

time—they belonged to a woman no longer in the first flush of youth, just the proper age to be the peasant's wife, but perhaps a trifle too attractive to be allowed out of the house when a stranger was around. Alaric shrugged painfully; if his host's intention had been so to exhaust him that he could feel no lust for any woman, let alone such a wife, the man had succeeded completely. Alaric went to the barn with his food and sat down stiffly beside Lightfoot, who was still nibbling hay. He was not surprised to hear the outside bolts shot home as the barn door closed behind him— the animals were snugly locked into individual stalls, but the human beast was not.

When he finished eating, he curled up in the hay with his own blanket, comfortably warm. He slept lightly, as usual, and no suspicious noises interrupted his slumber.

He was saddling his horse when the barn door unlocked and the peasant entered, carrying a small loaf of bread.

"May your journey be pleasant," he said, handing over the loaf. He had the scythe again, and a dagger at his waist as well, and he waved pointedly toward the road which led westward.

"You were going to tell me how much farther the forest continued to the west."

"Two days or three."

"When do I come into Durman territory?"

The peasant frowned. "The forest belongs to no one, that is all I know."

"And this inn is a half-day onward?"

"Yes."

"Is it large?"

"Large enough."

"Have you been there?"

"Once or twice."

"What is the owner's name?"

"Why do you ask?"

"Because I may seek work there, and I would like to know for whom to ask."

"His name, I believe, is Trif."

"Thank you, sir, and long life to you." Alaric mounted and spurred Lightfoot to a trot. He felt he had given a great deal of work for paltry food and less information, but tearing answers from the taciturn peasant was more than he cared to waste his time at. There was an inn ahead, down this winding trail, where, perhaps, folk would be more talkative. In any event, there would probably be a hearth, a soft bed, and an audience.

A white and gray dove flapped across the road in front of him, flying low to avoid branches and marauding hawks. Alaric viewed it as an omen of spring and new beginnings, and he began to hum.

The first indication that he was approaching an inn was a signpost at the right side of the road: a white rectangle upon which a black swan and an arrow pointing ahead were painted. Beneath, in large letters none too neatly drawn, were the words, "Inn of the Black Swan." Alaric puzzled them out slowly; Dall had known how to read and had taught his apprentice something of it, but it was still a slow process and a skill for which Alaric seldom found any use. His songs he had learned by listening to his master sing them over and over.

A short distance beyond the sign, a gust of north wind brought the scent of water to Alaric's nostrils—doubtless the river which the peasant had mentioned. A bit later, a side road branched off the main highway, and a second sign, identical to the first, marked it as leading to the inn. Near the mouth of the new road, a burly man, muffled in furs and scarves so that his face was quite invisible, was chopping down a tree, and when he saw Alaric, he suspended his activities and leaned on his axe.

"Good morrow," he said cheerily.

"Good morrow," said Alaric.

"You're a traveler?"

"That I am."

"All alone?"

"Yes, all alone."

"What, no other travelers on the road yet?"

"I haven't seen any. Is there truly an inn here?"

"Yes, there is, just as the sign says. If you doubt it, ride up this road a hundred paces, and you'll see the place."

"Do you work there?"

"I do."

"Is there a man named Trif who owns the place?"

The fellow cocked his head to one side. "There is a man named Trif. What would you want of him?"

"I would want a place as minstrel at the inn, but if there's no room for such, then honest work will do, for my horse and I must eat."

"It's a good man who thinks of his horse in the same breath as himself. I'm Trif, and if you'll come with me, I'll give you a meal in return for a song."

"A human being at last. My former host demanded that I chop wood."

Trif laughed. "We've plenty of hands for work here, but no voice worth a copper." He rested the axe on his shoulder and beckoned Alaric to follow him.

The Inn of the Black Swan was a tall structure of stone and wood, set in a wide clearing in which only a few tree trunks remained to indicate that it had once been part of the forest. Alaric tied his mount at a rail near the watering trough and, tucking his bedroll and

knapsack under either arm, strode with Trif through
the main entrance of the building.

Inside, the largest room on the first floor was furnished for dining with long tables and benches. The
hearth blazed cheerfully and, after settling his burdens
on a handy table, Alaric crossed the room to partake
of its warmth. Three people raised their heads in silent
greeting: two blond men playing draughts on a scarred
board before the fire and a dark-haired woman who
knelt, scrubbing the hearthstone. The minstrel smiled
amicably as he warmed his fingers. A moment later,
Trif—portly even divested of his bulky furs, with a
round, red face and a drooping black mustache—seated
himself in a nearby chair.

"So," he said, "as soon as you are ready, we will
judge your skill. These are Oldo and Gavver," indicating the draught players, "and Mizella," the
woman.

Seldom had he had so attentive an audience. As he
pulled himself up on a table and strummed a few notes
to loosen his fingers, the two men suspended their
game and sat still as two matching statues, elbows on
the board, chins cupped in their palms. The woman
pushed her soapy rags aside and sat down, legs drawn
up, feet tucked under her long skirt.

He sang about the brave travelers on the western sea
and how they fell over the edge of the world into fire
and mist. It was a sad song, perhaps not one he should
have chosen for a first impression, but he liked the
melody—indeed, it showed his voice off to best advantage, and his voice, better even than Dall's, was his
merchandise.

"I don't see why we shouldn't keep you," said
Trif. "Of course, you'll have to work like the rest of
us while the inn is empty, but when travelers come

by, you can consider minstrelsy your only occupation.''

"And when do travelers come by?''

"Once a week, perhaps, or more often as the weather improves. We are not at a great crossroads here, although boats do come down the river and stop with us as well as parties bound to and from Durman on the road. Between times, Oldo and Gavver hunt and trap; the rest of us—some, too, you haven't seen yet—care for the animals. And in the summer, Mizella has a garden. We are, you see, like a family, though not related to each other by blood, and each of us has some tale of woe that brought him here to no-man's-land. Perhaps you can compose some songs for us, eh?''

"One tale of woe is like another,'' Alaric replied. "Doubtless I have a song already that would fit each of you. But if someone should have a truly new complaint, I would gladly add it to my bag.''

"Come, sing another, and Mizella shall start supper while you entertain us.''

The woman rose obediently. She was eight or ten years older than the minstrel, small and light-boned, though well-proportioned, and she walked as softly as a cat. At the door to the kitchen, she paused, glanced back, and smiled at Alaric. She had a pretty face, and her lips in particular were beautifully formed. Alaric smiled back and sang about the milkmaid who married a prince and lived happily ever after. It was a shame, he reflected, that such things never happened in the real world.

Two men and four more women joined the group for supper. The women chattered among themselves in low voices, except for Mizella, who served the throng silently. Thorin and Wenk, the new men, smelled exactly like the pigs and goats they cared for. They clanked their trenchers, called the girls loud obscene names, and argued with each other so heatedly that at last Trif was obliged to shut them up by knocking their heads together. They settled down, then, muttering through clenched teeth instead of shouting.

When Mizella finally seated herself, it was opposite Alaric, and although she paid equal attention to the other men at the table, she seemed to reserve her most coquettish glances for him. He had half-formed plans for the night, wondering what she would say when she discovered he had no money, when a knife struck the table before him, its point sticking in the wood. He looked up sharply and saw Oldo towering over the far end of the board, his arm still outstretched.

"She is mine tonight, stranger," he said. His tone was bland, his expression completely without malice.

Trif was picking his teeth with a long thumbnail. "Come now, Oldo. He's just arrived, and she seems to fancy him."

"Let him take one of the others. She is spoken for."

"I would not wish to cause strife," said Alaric, rising from the table. "Permit me to retire alone."

"So be it." Trif pushed away from the board and motioned for the minstrel to follow him. They mounted a winding stairway at the rear of the room. Alaric looked back once and caught Mizella's eyes on him.

"When we have no guests, as now, you are welcome to sleep on the second floor," said Trif, "where the rooms are private and the beds soft and reasonably free of fleas and lice. The chamber of the green lozenge, to the left of the stairs, is not used by any of the others."

The bedroom upon whose door was painted a lopsided green diamond was tiny, cramped, and airless, and although the bed was soft, it was also musty.

"And where do you sleep when the inn is full?" asked Alaric.

"Upstairs in the loft."

"Then I choose the loft."

At the top of the stairway, one small, partly shuttered window shed late sunlight on a large open area crowded with boxes, barrels, and sacks. Hearthless— though the stones of the chimney showed in one wall— it was damp and chill, but less so than outdoors. The ceiling, merely the inside of the gabled roof, was missing a shingle or two, and puffs of cold air entered through the gaps to mingle with the equally frigid drafts from the window.

Alaric dropped his belongings in an empty corner; the sword, which had been wrapped in his blanket, slid half out of its handsome scabbard, clanking heavily against the bare floor.

Trif bent to look without touching it. "No shield or armor, yet you have a fine sword. Sir minstrel, would you be a knight as well?"

"No, indeed. The sword was a gift from a wealthy patron who thought I might have some use for it. He overestimated my skill, I fear, but I could not refuse."

"A squire, then. Perhaps you are too young to be a knight yet. Come, sir, I will keep your secret. Sent by the Lord of Durman to claim this territory for his crown? We have no law here; Durman's protection would be of great value to us all."

"I swear to you, I have no connection with Durman, nor am I either squire or knight, but simply a minstrel looking for his fortune."

Trif rocked back on his heels, hands clasped behind

himself. "You have great courage. Few men dare to travel these woods alone."

Alaric shrugged. "I knew nothing evil of these woods, therefore it took no courage to travel them."

"A cautious man might assume that robbers lurked in an unclaimed area."

"What robber would stop a traveler as threadbare as I?"

"Threadbare in cloth, perhaps," the landlord said. "Yet a man who wears such a sword must know how to use it, lest it be taken from him for its own sake."

Alaric smiled and shook his head. "I do not *wear* the sword. If I did, people would fear me. Where is the profit in that? Possibly I should sell it at my first opportunity and rid myself of an inconvenience that must be hidden in a bedroll, but I loved the one who gave it to me, and I cannot toss aside his gift so soon." He scooped a mound of straw into a single pallet and unrolled his blanket on top of it. "Your words imply that you need another arm; surely the five men you already have would be proof enough against the dangers of this forest, else you would not have the courage to stay here yourselves."

Trif shrugged. "Another sword would not be undesirable."

"I saw a peasant half a day's journey back easterly. His farm is lonely; is he not afraid?"

"I recall him, but my impression has been that he has nothing worth stealing."

Alaric forbore to mention the wife. If the peasant had wished his wife shown to the world, Trif would know what he had that was worth stealing.

"Here are candles," said the landlord, indicating a high shelf upon which rested a cracked dish and a stack of stubby, brownish cylinders. "If you should want something, go downstairs; someone will be watching the hearth all night.''

''I thank you.''

''Rest well.''

Alaric lay back on his pallet and watched the sky darken. He was lulled to sleep by muffled noises from the lower floors and by the soft cooing of doves in a small cot beside the window.

A rustling sound near his left ear roused him. Letting his eyelids lift slightly, he glanced around without moving his head. Someone—a woman, by her voluminous garb—was rummaging in his knapsack.

His first impulse was to flee; he quashed it, having learned a bit of self-restraint in recent months. Had the intruder been a man, he would not have been so tranquil, but a woman, weaponless as far as he could see, seemed less of a danger. He tried to think of what Dall would have done in such a situation. He corrected the thought: what Dall *had* done. He, himself, Alaric had been the thief, eleven years old, slipping a deft hand beneath Dall's mattress to purloin his silver. Dall had lain still, feigning sleep, and watched the child use his witch's power to escape with the money.

Alaric allowed the search to continue until he could hear the consternation in her movements, and then he said, ''You'll find nothing, for I haven't a copper.''

Rather than starting, she looked up slowly. Dim moonlight slanting through the half-open window revealed her face: Mizella.

''So I see,'' she said.

''A good thief makes less noise.''

''You sleep lightly.''

''Yes, when I sleep alone.''

''I apologize for trying to steal what you don't have.''

"You didn't believe I was a poor, starving minstrel?"

"No."

He touched her arm. "I will forgive your disbelief if you stay with me now. I can't pay you, but I can give you a song."

She laughed mirthlessly. "You think the others pay me?"

"*I* would if I could."

"*Customers* pay. Trif says you are to be one of us."

"For a while. I don't know how long."

"We all came here for a while . . . and here we are still. That is how things happen in the forest. If you stay long, you will stay forever."

"It would be pleasant to stay if there were something to keep me."

"As for that," she murmured, "I couldn't say," and slid into his arms.

At breakfast, he was still puzzling over her behavior. Stealing from patrons he could understand; they might not notice the theft until the inn was far behind them, and then, if it were only a matter of a few coppers, they might shrug it off as not worth returning for. But stealing from one's fellow workers, members of the same household, was a different—and more foolish—matter. It was bound to cause discord. Yet Trif's actions at dinner the previous night indicated strongly that he allowed little discord in his "family."

It was not mere theft, then. Mizella, shaking out every fold of cloth, probing every corner of his knapsack, had been searching for something. She, or more probably all of them, did not trust him, suspected he was more than he admitted. And they were afraid, else they would never bother with such a blatant investigation. She had even peered at his clothes while undressing him.

Afraid of what? What could one lone man possibly do, trapped in a house full of armed defenders? The landlord had spoken of robbers and of the desirability of Durman claiming this forest, lending its protection. Were there, perhaps, gangs whose scouts insinuated themselves into the good graces of a household and then attacked from the rear as their cohorts attacked from the front? But what could they have been looking for in his knapsack that would identify him as such a scout? Hidden wealth? Weapons? He decided to end his uncertainty by asking point-blank.

"What were you searching for last night, Mizella?"

Everyone at the table looked up, and the abrupt cessation of chatter was startling.

Mizella shrugged. "I don't know. I would have recognized it if I'd found it."

"And you didn't find it?"

"No, minstrel, I didn't find anything."

Alaric glanced sharply at the landlord. "Then are you satisfied that I am what I say I am?"

Trif smiled slowly. "No man is what he says he is."

"Well, I'm not a villain, come to murder you in your beds!"

"No? Ah, I feel much better now you've said that." He laughed and scooped up the last of his porridge. "Come outside, minstrel, and I'll show you a few things that need to be done for the common comfort. And we won't even mount a guard on you."

The laugh seemed genuine enough, and Alaric decided that he must have passed whatever test had been administered. If the forest were as dangerous as Trif insisted, he could hardly blame the man for entertaining some suspicions about a stranger.

Alaric was assigned some light tasks which passed

the time agreeably enough. In the course of accomplishing them, he pried into every room of the inn, memorizing details of their arrangement, storing the information in his capacious memory almost without conscious effort. After dinner he played a pair of songs for the whole company.

Mizella came to his pallet again, earlier this night. "I told Oldo you asked for me. I'll make a bed in the other corner if you prefer to sleep alone."

"Whatever you like. I have no hold over you."

"Then I'll stay here."

"I thank you for the flattery. Do you find me a better lover than Oldo?"

"I don't know yet, but I like a man who doesn't order me about."

"How can I order you about when I hardly know you?"

She shrugged. "I'm a whore."

"A man who pays nothing has little right to make demands."

"The others pay nothing, yet I *am* paid, in the food I eat, the roof over my head, and the clothes I wear. If you stay long and add your share to the common pot, you'll be paying me, too."

"How did such a pretty girl as you come to a wilderness place like this? I would think to see you with a strong husband and fat children."

"Now you ask for a tale of woe, minstrel. Did you not say you had heard them all?"

"And I also said I was always open to a new complaint."

"You'll find nothing new here. Once, I lived with my parents and my brothers and sisters on a large manor. We farmed, as did all our neighbors, and it was neither a pleasant nor an unpleasant life. As the eldest, it was my duty to carry the excess milk to market one day a week. Our marketplace was the manor courtyard, and there, sitting in a high seat, the lord would oversee the bartering and resolve disputes among his vassals. He was a large man, with great shoulder muscles from swinging a sword and carrying heavy armor, and his face was always red. I first saw him when I was very little, and he was just the same then as ten years later.

"Well, I came of an age to marry. The suitor my parents chose for me was ugly and a fool—when he came round our hut, I threw clods of dung to drive him away. Truly, there wasn't a man in the district, either married or free, that I would have taken as a husband, but *that* one especially I hated. My parents argued and screamed and beat me, but that only made me more certain of my mind. At last, the lord of the manor came one night, drove my mother and father out of our home, and talked to me alone. I had often seen his eyes on me in the marketplace, but I had never dared to speak to him; yet there he was, not three paces away from me, sitting on our best chair—our only chair, in fact—whispering to me. And of what did he speak? Of the delights of his bed that awaited me when he claimed his right of the first night of my marriage. *That*, he said, would be worth wedding an ugly fool. Bah!

"I pretended to change my mind, and everyone was happy. I could see his lordship sweating lust for me as he took his leave. In a few days, he thought, he would bed me. But when my parents slept that night, I left with just the clothes on my back, not even taking the new chemise my mother had woven for me.

"I ran, and when I could not run, I walked as quickly as possible, and by daybreak I was on a strange road, among strange fields. I wandered, offering to work for my meals and lodging, begging when I had

to. Many people were kind—when I told them I was
an orphan. Still, it was not long before I lost my vir-
ginity. I had to eat.''

''Trif?''

''No. I don't remember the man. It was ten years
ago, I think, or perhaps nine. I met Trif only last winter, in a town in Durman, and he persuaded me to
come here with him and join his 'family.' ''

''Not my notion of a family.''

''The men remind me of my brothers, who always
fought at the table until my father cuffed them. And
now: what calamities have brought you to this outpost
of nowhere?''

He was stretched out on his back now, one arm
around her, her head cradled in the crook of his elbow.
He looked for a moment toward the window, where
the gibbous moon was just peeking over the sill. As
once or twice before, he had the urge to confide the
whole truth to her willing ears, to tell of his childhood
experiments with the witch's power, to reflect aloud
on the mystery of his origin. Not since Dall died had
he done so, and the secrets bottled up inside him
throbbed to be set free. Yet the scent of danger was
strong; to bed a woman was not to know her—Dall
had said that once. Mizella, whose dark tresses lapped
across his chest, was a stranger. He censored his saga,
then censored it more heavily as he realized that a
woman, even a whore, might not appreciate certain of
his exploits.

''It must be sweet,'' she said when he had finished,
''to have a gift like yours, to be welcome everywhere
because you have something that no one else can offer.''

''There are other minstrels.''

''A few. But when I think of how many women
there are . . . all I can offer is my body, and any

wench has that. If I were a minstrel, people would value me as more than a hole to be filled. Oh, teach me your art! I swear to bed with you every night if you will!''

'If I did, I would soon find myself without employment: an inn scarcely needs more than one minstrel.'' He laughed softly, then his voice became serious. ''There is no fortune in such a life; I haven't a copper to my name, as you well know. One must learn to sing and to play the lute or some other, easily portable instrument, and one must carry a thousand songs in his memory—not the simplest task in the world.''

''You have done it.''

''To be sure, but one must have a natural inclination as well as a desire to learn. One's voice must be pure and flexible, his fingers nimble and deft.''

''Ah, minstrel, let me try. Give me a lesson.''

''Stubborn woman. Tomorrow, then. Not tonight, lest we wake the household; I need no quarrel with your 'brothers' to ease my rest.''

''Sweet minstrel. Let me kiss you.''

He let her do more than that.

Sunny midmorning found Alaric finished with his earliest tasks and settled by the hearth with his flute. Gavver was there, tending the fire and whittling a new set of draughtsmen, standing watch in case some customer arrived. The other men were gone; after breakfast, Trif had climbed to the loft to feed the doves, his morning habit, and returned with a bundle of broadbladed hunting arrows—a silent indication of his plans for the day. Alaric had pleaded ineptitude, and the landlord did not press him to join the party.

A hand on his shoulder startled him. Mizella. Intent on his song, he had not heard her approach.

"Now?" she said. She carried a dusty lute by the neck.

"Ah, where was *that* hiding?" Alaric wondered.

"Up in the storeroom. It's different from yours."

"Yes, well, I made mine myself, and it is not quite a true lute. Yours has a rose, as it should." He pointed to the intricately carved pattern of perforations in the center of the new-found instrument's sounding board. His own bore a simple round hole instead. "I had too little patience. The tone is fuller, I think, with the large hole, though the other is prettier. And without the rose, a coin dropped inside shakes out much easier."

Mizella's brow wrinkled. "What is *that?*"

"What?"

Her fingers dipped between the strings and plucked from the innards of his lute a length of black cloth which was embroidered in red, blue, and purple.

"A kerchief," he replied.

"How beautiful. Loving fingers did this work."

"Yes. Yes, they did."

"Your mother?"

"No. A friend." He took it from her, tucked it back inside. "You're ready for your lesson now?"

She sat at his feet, cradling the dusty lute in her lap. She traced an idle design in the grime. "Yes, my lesson."

"Well, first you must be able to sing. Without that, the best lute-playing in the world is worthless. Sing for me."

She looked down at the floor. "I don't know any songs."

"What, none at all? A child's song, surely. A simple rhyme. No? Well, then, I'll teach you one:

> *Over the river and over the hill*
> *And over the moon I fly*

To foreign lands and silver sands
While safe in my bed I lie.

Come, sing it with me.''

She tried. She tried several times, but the result was less than satisfactory. She had no ear for music and lost the melody with ease, improvising her own—quite out of tune—and thinking it the same as the original.

After considerable time, Alaric called a halt. ''I don't know. Perhaps it will come with practice, but perhaps one must be caught young. I was eleven when I began.''

''I am . . . quite a bit older than eleven.''

She said that in such a forlorn tone that the minstrel looked up sharply to search her face for some reason. Her eyes were downcast, and for the first time, he saw tiny crow's feet at their corners. She would never pass for eighteen, certainly, but there was youth in her smile and in her step, and she was more than a decade younger than Dall had been when he died. Yet, there was despair in her voice, as if her life were almost over.

He reached out and took her hand. ''And much more attractive than if you were only eleven.''

She shrugged.

''Perhaps you'll have better luck with your fingers.''

She shook her head, pulling away from him. ''I have work waiting for me in the kitchen. Another time, minstrel.''

''If that's what you wish.''

She walked toward the kitchen, hips swaying, but she stopped halfway across the room and turned. ''Is she still alive?''

''Who?''

She pointed toward his lute, which was propped up

against a chair. "The friend who gave you the ker-chief."

"As far as I know, yes."

"Young?"

"Near my own age."

"Not a sister?"

"No."

"You love her?"

Alaric touched the neck of his lute, drew a murmur of sound from one string. "I will probably never see her again," he replied. He looked away as Mizella walked on to the kitchen.

He was still by the fire when the hunting party returned, bearing not deer and rabbits but boxes and bundles, which they silently took up to the loft.

"A strange hunt," Alaric said to Trif.

"Oh, we saw a boat on the river and quickly traded our game for things we can't get so easily. When one lives in the wilderness, one must take advantage of every opportunity that presents itself."

"Indeed, how fortunate you were, then, that a boat happened to pass when you had a substantial supply of meat to offer."

Trif smiled. "Yes. How fortunate."

The smallest container was opened that evening and produced a tablecloth, linen napkins, and fine steel knives for carving the dinner joint. Perhaps in celebration of these acquisitions, the entire company had scattered to their private stores to effect a transformation for the meal. Trif, at the head of the table, sported a white shirt trimmed with lace at throat and wrist. His fellows wore hand-tooled belts, colorful silken scarves, and slender silver hoops as earrings and bracelets. They ate and chattered with a gusto greater than usual.

Mizella was the last to enter and seat herself for

dinner. She had put on a fresh dress and combed her hair back, the better to show off a chain of intricate gold filigree about her neck.

"What a lovely piece of workmanship," Alaric said as she sat down beside him. He touched the necklace, lifted it, found it feather-light. "I marvel at the number of carcasses this must have cost."

"None. It was a gift."

"Then you've had rich guests at this forlorn spot."

"We have," she replied, and then a startled expression passed over her face. She turned slowly and stared at Oldo, who sat on her opposite side. Her lips compressed to whiteness, and with slow deliberation she picked up her water glass, took a single sip of its contents, and splashed the rest in his face.

Oldo sprang to his feet, almost upsetting the table, and seized Mizella by the hair.

"Be thankful it wasn't red wine, you oaf!" she shouted.

Trif halted the clash with a word, and the combatants sank into an uneasy truce which was punctuated only by silent glares of anger.

Later, the diners paired off and drifted upstairs, leaving the landlord, Alaric, and Mizella alone.

"Go on to bed, minstrel. Mizella and I have words to exchange in private." Trif was circling the room, extinguishing the hanging lights.

Alaric shrugged; he felt no claim on the woman. Bidding them good night, he picked a brand from the fire for a torch and started toward the stairs. At the first landing, he stopped. The voices that drifted upward from the main room were low, the words unintelligible, but the tone was angry. He crushed the brand with his foot and moved silently back down the stairs until, kneeling, he could see into the room.

They were standing by the hearth. Trif had Mizella

by one arm, and as he spoke, he shook her, though not violently. His attitude was too benign to imply danger but too menacing for love.

Alaric scanned the hall. Only firelight remained to illuminate it, and the shadows were deep. Behind the table, particularly—where the darkness cast by the fine new cloth was as absolute as any in the forest—was the perfect spot from which to listen to their conversation. Instantly, he was there.

Now the voices were clear, and Alaric could see the speakers through the gap left where the tablecloth did not quite reach the floor.

"If he ever *ever* kicks me under the table again, I will not let you keep me from scratching his eyes out!" Mizella was saying.

"Little fool, you trust this minstrel too much too soon. You saw how quickly he noticed the difference of degree between a new shirt and a gold necklace. A good thing it was that Oldo warned you to shut your mouth. Do you think that all this time I have been trying to convince him that we are *rich?*"

"If he hasn't seen what's in the loft by now—"

"Bah! The loft is nothing. Would I let *him* sleep there if there were anything left to see?"

"He is an innocent boy, nothing more. He won't cause any trouble. I would stake my life on it."

"I don't care if you stake your own life on it, but *my* life means a great deal to me. Therefore, you will hide your little baubles for a while longer yet, unless you've already shown them all." He twisted her arm a little, and she grimaced in pain.

"No, nothing else. Tonight was the first time."

"You're getting clumsy with this 'innocent boy,' Mizella. Perhaps talking a bit too much? I have trusted you, Mizella; don't betray that trust!"

"Let go of me. I've said nothing I shouldn't say."

He released her arm, and she rubbed the marks his fingers left. "He is very sweet and very young, and I feel motherly toward him."

"Motherly?" He laughed. "Well, then, go to your incestuous bed, little mother, and bear in mind what we've said here."

She turned away angrily and strode toward the stairway.

Alaric was lying on his pallet, pretending to be half asleep, when she reached the loft. She molded her body to his back, and he felt the necklace biting into his shoulder.

"I thought you were staying with Trif," he yawned.

"I make my own choices," she replied, and her hands began to move on him.

Much later, they were still awake. Alaric toyed lazily with her hair, twining the strands around his fingers, brushing them across his cheek. He thought about the hearthside conversation, heard it once again in the ears of his mind, and wondered when, if ever, Trif would really relinquish the suspicions that prowled behind that smiling facade. Of the whole household, only Mizella seemed to accept him unreservedly. Did she truly feel maternal toward him? From his present, naked viewpoint, he could hardly credit it. But the notion made him curious.

"I have been thinking of your 'family' here," he said. "It seems strange that with all these . . . affectionate women in the household, there should be no children. Had you stayed with a peasant husband on your lord's manor, you'd have half a dozen by now, clinging to your skirts at every turn."

"I have borne children." He could not see her expression in the dark, but there was a curious flatness to her voice.

"What happened to them?"

She hesitated a long time before replying, and when she spoke, it was in a barely audible tone. "I lived in hovels, in soldiers' barracks, sometimes even in ditches. I had no home, no family, no skill but one, if that can be called a skill. I learned quickly that chance acquaintances care little for squalling babes, and so a whore encumbered by children eats less often than one who is not. I told myself I could only feed one mouth with the pittance I earned at my trade. I wish I could see your face now—do you think me an unnatural mother?"

"Did you kill them?"

She sat up suddenly; her silhouette was a dark blotch against the moonlit window. "Kill them? I carried them in my body; how could I kill them? No! I wrapped them up against the night chill and left them as foundlings. I left them and ran. . . . Ah, minstrel, they screamed and cried, but they were my babies."

He touched her arm, followed it upward to her hand, which was covering her face. "Many?"

"Two. A boy and a girl. They would be seven and eight now, and they don't even know their mother."

"Would they be happy as a whore's children?"

"Are they happy now? Are they even *alive?* At least if I had kept them, I would *know.*"

He sat up, put his arm around her. "Perhaps you did the best thing."

"A man cannot understand how a woman feels, especially a very young man. Years ago, I felt as you do. I didn't care about them; they were a yoke around my neck."

"Then why do you care now?"

"Because there won't be any more children for me." She bent her head against his shoulder. "I was sick some years ago, and after that . . . barren."

He stroked her hair.

"When I was younger, I thought that someday I would not be a whore any more. I dreamed of a tall handsome man who would take me away with him to a land of happiness. A childish dream. Even if such a man existed—a man who could forget my past—a man wants sons, and *those* I can never give." She sighed deeply.

"Sons are not everything," said Alaric.

"I was a daughter, and I know how much his sons meant to my father."

"A man who wanted you for your own sweet self would not care about sons."

"You have a heart, minstrel, for speaking so even though you know what I have done."

"I cannot pass judgment on you. I was abandoned as a child, left on a hillside to die beneath the cold moon, and who is to say that my fate would have been better if my parents had kept me? Perhaps my mother, too, was a whore and thought much as you did. If so, I thank her for it. My life has not been a smooth one, but I have memories I would not part with." He lay back, pulling her with him. "Is there a person alive, I wonder, who would not change the past if he could? I have a thousand songs on that theme."

Mizella pressed closer. "You are very wise for one so young."

"Not nearly as wise as I wish. And if you call me 'young' once more, I shall be forced to demonstrate my maturity."

"Yes, do. You make me forget that I'm an evil old hag."

He made love to her gently, then, for she was weeping.

* * *

The days passed easily, and as the weather warmed, more and more of the household activities were extended out-of-doors. The men began construction of a new chicken house to replace the old one, which had barely survived the winter even though it had been in a sheltered spot behind the small barn. The women laundered and mended clothing, hanging it to air in the light breeze that blew continuously from the river.

One particular day, Alaric's task was to shape shingles for the roof of the inn, to cover those chinks through which the winter gale had entered the loft. He lazed on a bench that circled the well in the rear courtyard, his back against roughly dressed stones, his feet propped up on a stump. He worked sporadically, his attention constantly diverted by nearby movement: Gavver splitting rails for the new coop; a curious fox peeking out of the woods; a gray dove flapping about the roof before settling in the dovecot. A disorderly stack of finished shingles grew beside him; occasionally, the topmost one would slide off and clatter to the ground—after the third time, he left it where it lay.

Mizella was scrubbing floors. He had watched her all morning as she made regular trips outside to toss dirty water into the woods and draw fresh buckets at the well. She smiled at him and ruffled his hair with one hand while turning the crank with the other. Once, she kissed his forehead.

He was pleased with the sight of her and yet not pleased at all. Her walk was a silent, barefoot dance that reminded him of her lithe, boneless movements of the dark hours. She had come to him every night, ignoring the other men, ignoring their pointed glances, their suggestive whispers, even their blunt queries. She clung to him as if he were her man, and that disturbed him. In spite of his protestations, he knew in his heart that he *was* too young—too young for a woman like her. Certainly too young and too weak to hold her if someone else wanted her. Very obviously, Oldo wanted her. It was only a matter of time before he lost patience and offered to fight. Sword to sword, knife to knife—Alaric knew who would lose *that* game. Oldo had a scar or two on his face, and the way he had tossed a knife the very first night of their acquaintance left no doubt that he had ten times the experience of a sixteen-year-old minstrel.

Mizella was a puzzle. That she loved him, he could not quite believe. She had seen too much of life to swoon over a stripling boy, even though he listened kindly to her sorrows and tumbled her in a satisfactory manner. Nor could he believe that maternal emotions could inspire such physical desire. His songs—that vast reservoir of unrequited passion and rueful hindsight—suggested she was using him to make another jealous. Oldo? She hated him vigorously—was that merely the obverse of love? Did she realize her behavior was likely to tear the household apart?

Yet when he saw her smile, he felt it was not a false or calculated smile, and when she came to him at night, her hunger seemed as real as hunger had ever been.

He did not love her. He had never said he loved her. He supposed that many a casual bedmate had mouthed such words in her ear, meaning nothing by them, but his compassion forbade it. He liked her, found her skilled and lovely, but, primarily, he was using her—and, indeed, his whole existence at the inn—as a defense in his battle against a dreamland of might-have-been to which he dared not yield. To maintain that defense, to keep the household running smoothly and himself a part of it, he would very soon have to insist that she mollify Oldo. He wondered what she would say to that.

He was on the roof nailing a shingle into place when he heard a number of human voices and snorting, plodding horses in the yard below. Inching his way to the peak of the gable, he looked down and saw Trif leading a party of men toward the inn. He counted five strangers and four extra pack animals, heavily laden. Thinking he would be wanted soon, Alaric scrambled to the ladder and met Oldo, who had been dispatched to call him.

"Trif says to clean up and come entertain the guests."

Alaric drew a bucket of water from the well, washed hastily, and headed for the main hall, where he had left his lute earlier in the day.

Mizella caught him at the kitchen doorway; she held the instrument in her arms. "I picked it up just before they came in. I thought you wouldn't want them handling it."

"Exactly," he said, squeezing her shoulder gratefully.

"I can't come to you tonight. The guests. . . ."

"Of course."

"Perhaps very late. . . ."

"Won't the others be sleeping up in the loft tonight? We wouldn't have much privacy."

She looked over her shoulder into the large room. "Yes. Yes, that's true." Then she brushed past him and joined the other women at food preparation.

The new arrivals had shed their cloaks and caps and were gathered around a table near the fire by the time Alaric entered the room. They were ruddy-cheeked outdoor men of varying ages, and three of them resembled each other enough to be brothers. They talked of their route beyond the forest, into

Durman, and one man was sketching an imaginary map on the tabletop. They looked up as the minstrel drew near.

"Good eve, fair sirs," he said. "May I offer a song while you wait for the fine dinner I have just seen being prepared for you?"

"What's this—a minstrel?" cried the eldest man. "Why, one would think this inn at the center of the world instead of its edge."

"I saw a couple of wenches in the kitchen, too, Derol," said one of his companions. "I hope they don't tire quickly."

Alaric grinned as he perched himself atop the next table, his feet on its bench.

"A song. Surely, a song," said Derol.

The minstrel obliged, and soon he had them listening eagerly to a rather long saga concerning an enchanted prince who fell in love with the young witch who had laid the spell upon him; too late, the hapless noble discovered that the only means of nullifying the enchantment was to destroy the enchantress, and so he ended his days as a rooster in her farmyard, preferring such a fate to the murder of his beloved. At the finish of the tale, the travelers immediately launched into a discussion of what each of them would do if confronted with the same situation; only the youngest, who was not much older than Alaric, maintained that the prince had acted properly.

"You'll learn, my boy," said Derol, "after you've been in and out of love a time or two. No woman's worth giving up your life for."

"He didn't give up his life," the youngster pointed out.

"He gave up his *human* life, which, in my eyes, is quite the same thing. Am I right, minstrel?"

"I prefer to sing the song and allow the listener to interpret it as he will."

"Oho, a slippery fellow," said the man who had mentioned females in the kitchen. "He'll live a long time by refusing to take sides in an argument."

At that moment, the five women of the household entered, each bearing a steaming platter heaped high with meat and vegetables. Trif brought up the rear with a tray of bread trenchers and metal cups and a jug of fragrant wine.

The women served, giggling all the while—even Mizella, who was normally the soberest of the lot. They had eaten earlier, and now they could lavish their attentions on the customers, chattering gaily, joking, smiling open invitations. Before the meal ended, each had chosen and confirmed her man for the night. Mizella paired off with Derol, who balanced her on his lap while he quaffed his second cup of wine.

Alaric found his own, less engrossing skills ignored, and he drifted away from the boisterous group soon after the meal was served. In the kitchen, he found Oldo, Gavver, and Wenk quietly attacking a dinner slightly less sumptuous than that offered the guests. He shut his lute into a high, empty cabinet—where no clumsy fingers were likely to disturb it—and joined them. Though the kitchen door was snugly shut, they could still hear the merriment of the main room. Their meal was disposed of and an entire round of draughts between Oldo and Gavver completed before the din receded, signifying that the diners were retiring for the night.

Trif came into the kitchen. He carried the wine jug. "They've gone upstairs." Tilting the carafe to his lips, he drained the last drops of fluid. "Clear the table, and then you can all go to bed."

Up in the loft, the four men who did not habitually

sleep there made themselves straw pallets. The landlord remained downstairs, watching at the hearth.

Alaric fell asleep quickly.

A wild, piercing shriek woke him.

At first, he thought it the scream of some animal in
the woods, perhaps a cat in heat. Then, when he realized he was alone in the loft, he knew it for a human
cry, though he had never heard such a sound issue
from a human throat before. He groped for his boots
and his sword.

Pausing at the top of the stairs, he listened. Below,
the building was silent, except for some muffled noises
that might be amorous couples moving in their beds
or might be only the wind. A few faint but rhythmic
footsteps echoed, as if someone were trying to pace
away the boredom of insomnia. The commotion which
would surely have ensued if someone had fallen,
screaming, from a window or merely awakened from
a nightmare with that horrifying cry on his lips was
absent.

Yet something had lured his loft companions from
their slumber.

He gripped the sword with sweaty fingers and cautiously descended three steps. A board squeaked
loudly under his feet, and he froze, waiting for some
reaction to that small sound, waiting for a voice to
challenge him. Nothing happened. Had he, perhaps,
wakened long after the shriek—merely *thinking* that
he had wakened immediately—long after the rest of
the household and the guests had dashed off to investigate, leaving only one or two of their number to
guard the hearth? Was the inn so silent because it
was almost empty?

Or was the real reason uglier than that?

Alaric thought of the brigands the landlord had
feared. Perhaps, in the depths of darkness before

moonrise, they had fallen on the inn, murdered the men, raped the women. Perhaps the shriek had been a cry of mortal agony torn from Trif's own throat. Alaric peered into the gloom of the stairwell but could not penetrate it. He was afraid to descend, afraid that the inn was in cruel, enemy hands and that he would be plunging, unarmored and alone, indifferently trained in the martial arts, into their midst. He imagined arrows, spears, swords, and knives, all pointed toward himself, and his faith in his witch's agility was not strong enough to propel him downward. His heart hammered wildly. No longer could he stand, unshielded, at the head of the stairs, a perfect target silhouetted against the faintly lit loft.

He was at the bench beside the well, alone but for his sword and the long shadow cast him by the moon.

The inn was dark except for a knife's edge of illumination beneath the kitchen door. Alaric crept closer, flattened his body to the ground, and attempted to peer into the room through the narrow crevice. He saw a floor-sweeping skirt. A moment later, several pairs of boots came into his field of vision, and he retreated apprehensively to the cover of the well.

The door opened, and Wenk and Gavver emerged, carrying between them a bulky, cloth wrapped bundle. Oldo and Thorin followed closely with a similar burden. They passed near Alaric, who circled the well to keep out of sight, and entered the forest.

Mizella had held the door for them; chancing that she would be companionless now, Alaric knocked softly, standing aside so that he could not be seen from the room's interior. The stout oaken panel swung back slightly, and Mizella peeked out.

"Are you alone?" he whispered.

She started at the sound of his voice. "How did you get outside?"

"Are you *alone?*"

"Well, yes, for now."

"Will they be back soon?"

"No, not too soon."

"Where's Trif?"

"Upstairs."

"All right." He slipped into the kitchen and closed the door securely behind him.

"You were in the loft, and Trif is watching the stairs. How did you get outside?"

"I climbed out the window."

"Did they see you?"

"No."

"You've got to go back, pretend you were never out, pretend you slept the whole night. Please, you *have* to."

"Why? What's going on. I heard a scream—"

Mizella moaned and sank back against the work-table, which was still piled high with dinner's refuse. "I knew you'd hear it. Oh, please, take your horse and go, right now. Don't stop for anything. I won't tell them I saw you. With luck, they won't look in the loft till . . . till dawn." She caught sight of the sword, half-hidden behind his right thigh. "You can't hold them off. There's only one of you. *Please.*"

His free hand clutched her shoulder. *"What is going on?"*

"They're killing the travelers. Now will you go before they find you?"

"Too late for that, my dear," said Trif, stepping through the door from the dining room. "You whisper a bit too loudly." He carried a sword in one hand and a bloody dagger in the other.

"No, Trif, no, he's just a boy," Mizella cried, clinging to Alaric. "Nothing more, just a boy!"

"I am still not convinced of that. In any event,

knight, squire, or nothing, we simply cannot trust him. Nor you, I fear, now that you feel so strongly about him."

Mizella paled. "I wish he *were* a Durman knight, sent to discover what happened to all those travelers who never arrived at their destinations."

"The world is cruel," Trif replied. "Crueler than even you, my fluff, can imagine." He crossed the floor in two sudden steps, sword raised high.

Alaric lifted his blade in a desperate, awkward parry of the stroke an armored man would meet with his shield. He had no shield save Mizella, a fleshly, too vulnerable covering for his left side. Trif's dagger snaked toward her middle as his sword slid against Alaric's, its point tilted downward for a thrust.

The minstrel locked his free arm about Mizella's waist and threw himself backward, lifting her clear of the floor and slamming both of their bodies into the unyielding kitchen door. Thinking them trapped and off balance, Trif lunged forward to follow through with his two thrusts . . . and met empty air.

The forest sprang up around Alaric and Mizella.

Alaric's sword fell from his numbed fingers, thudding twice as it hit the ground tip first, then hilt. He held Mizella tightly, afraid that if he let her go she would crumple. He had never carried another human being when he traveled in his special way; the extra instant of concentration he had allowed for enveloping her with his power might have been too long, might have let Trif's dagger reach her. Or it might have been too short and left part of her body behind. A long moment passed before he could bring himself to face the possibly gruesome truth.

"Mizella," he whispered.

He felt a violent tremor pass through her body.

"Are you injured?"

Her voice was tiny, muffled by his shoulder. "No."

He relaxed then, loosened his grip on her waist, and let her toes touch the earth. "We're safe now."

She raised her head, gazing at him with terror-wide eyes.

"There's nothing to fear," he told her.

She pushed his encircling arm aside and moved a few steps back. Above, she saw the moon peeking through high branches, and at her feet, gnarled roots and the moist fragments of winter's waning snowdrifts. All about were numberless trees; she stared at them as if trying to read some message in their shadowy forms. "Where are we?" she whispered.

"On the road about half a day's journey east of the inn."

She spun around to face him. "Am I dreaming, or . . . *what are you?*"

"Don't be afraid of me, Mizella." He stretched a hand toward her, palm outward, as if warding off a blow.

"You're a witch."

He planted his left foot firmly on the hilt of his sword, which lay on the ground between them. He didn't want her to try anything rash. "I have a certain talent that other people lack," he admitted. "But I prefer to use it as little as possible."

"A witch." In the darkness, he could barely see her hug herself with crossed arms. "I've touched a witch, kissed, bedded—"

"Mizella, no! A minstrel, a boy, just as you said. Nothing more. If it hadn't meant our lives, you would never have known I was anything else. Don't think of me as a witch."

"But I must; you are!" She fell at his feet, clasping his knees. "Let me serve you, lord!"

Thrown off balance, he staggered and caught at her wrists to right himself. "What?"

"I am not afraid."

"Get up, Mizella; the ground is cold and damp."

"Don't turn me away, lord. There's blood on my hands already; I won't shy from your bidding!"

"What are you saying?" He stepped back, but she crawled after, clinging to his legs.

"I'm a murderess, as surely as if I'd killed them myself."

"Who? The travelers?"

"Yes! Those of last night and others—many others! Did you think this was the first time we'd slain our guests as they lay sated and sleeping? The river and the road were our domain, and the travelers who were too rich now lie scattered through the forest in unmarked graves. My necklace, that you liked so well, was the gift of a dead man!"

He had assumed. . . . He wasn't sure that he had assumed anything during those fleeting moments of battle—his mind had been too occupied with escape for rational thought. His arms, his flesh, his bones had decided that whatever had happened, Mizella, who warned him of the danger, was faultless. The notion that she was a consenting part of an elaborate scheme to waylay hapless travelers jarred him, and he searched for some shred of the innocence he had supposed.

"But *yourself,* you killed none."

"No, I lulled them with my body till Trif could come upstairs and slit their throats. Is that not close enough to murder? Lord, I have the courage to perform any evil deed you would require!"

"Stop calling me lord!" He jerked her to her feet and picked up the sword, over which she had heedlessly scrambled in her haste to hold him fast. "This bloody work—did you enjoy it?"

She glanced at the naked blade, then tried to back away, but he gripped her forearm securely. "Please . . . I tried to save your life . . . please. . . ."

"I shall not forget that. Answer the question."

"I've heard of witches . . . that they always see a lie."

"Then speak the truth."

Her voice quavered as she said, "At first, I didn't know. Trif said a home, permanent employment, no more lying in ditches or dark alleys. There was no talk of murder. But later, there *was* murder—butchery of sleeping men. I confess I didn't like it. I tried to run away—three or four times—but they always caught me. I was . . . punished, and after a few punishments, I did as I was told, whatever it was."

"What did they do to you?"

"Beat me, burned me, especially my back. The scars don't show when my clothes are on, and in the dark, no one would notice."

He felt sudden, sympathetic pains, but he maintained a stern demeanor. "And the answer to my question?"

"The travelers were nothing to me, nothing but bodies in the darkness, all with the same groans of pleasure, the same sweat. They were nothing. . . . But still, I could not help thinking that they were men with families somewhere, families that waited for them forever. Lord, I can't answer your question any better than that."

His fingers fell away from her.

"Lord, I have had a kindly thought or two. Who has not? But a woman who would desert her own children is surely evil enough for your purposes."

He sighed. "What do you know of my purposes?"

"Please . . . if you forsake me, I have nowhere else to turn."

"Why did you warn me? You could have stayed where you were, safe as a bear in its winter den. You could have slammed the door in my face, screamed for Trif, betrayed me and been exactly as you were before."

"No. You were a boy, I thought, too young to be involved in such a grisly game. And Trif was too sure Durman had sent you to spy; eventually, he would have killed you. Had I known you were a witch, I would not have worried so." She paused. "A witch in Durman's pay?"

"As suspicious as your former master!"

"The murderer sees a knife behind every tree."

Ah, we have something in common, he thought, but he did not say it aloud. "Well, I am not in Durman's pay, as I've said before, nor in anyone else's."

"The Dark One pays well enough, I should think."

"Nor in the Dark One's."

"How not? You're a witch!"

"Let us settle this matter now: I cast no spells, lay no curses, and make no potions. I have no evil tasks for you to perform and I *want* none, so you can stop trying to convince me of your desirability as a servant."

"None at all?"

"None at all."

"You're testing me."

"No."

"You're . . . a good witch?" The turmoil in her mind was evident in her voice.

"Neither good nor bad. I am a minstrel, and I have no desire to be otherwise. What happened tonight, you must forget. Come, I'm chilled to the bone. We're not far from the hut of a peasant I once chopped wood for;

surely he'll let us sleep in his barn in return for a bit of work. Then tomorrow, we'll travel afoot southward, as far as we can, and in the night, when the household has settled down, I'll go back for my lute and my horse.''

''Wait; this peasant lives a half-day's journey east of the inn?''

''Yes.''

''Then I know him. He must not see me.''

''Why not?''

''In return for a share of the booty, four families watch the road and the river for Trif. They greet unwary horsemen and boatmen, recommending that they stop at the inn; then they free a dove, which flies home to its birthplace, the dovecot in the loft. A notched thong tied to the bird's leg tells how many travelers and which direction they come from. A black thong is a call for help, and if he did nothing else, your peasant would surely dispatch *that* as soon as he caught sight of me, for he knows that I am not allowed away from the inn.''

''A well-organized forest this is!''

''Trif is no fool. If he trusts these people, then we cannot.''

Alaric sighed and took her arm to guide her southward. ''Then we'll begin our travels now and hope that walking heats our blood.''

''Where are we going?''

''Out of the forest. After that, I don't know. Shall I take you back to your parents?''

''No, please, not that. What would they do with a whore but spit on her?''

''What shall I do with you, then?''

''Let me be your companion.''

He made no immediate reply.

Her fingers tightened on his arm. ''I see . . . I was

wrong. You're truly not—what I thought. Not like the tales old women tell late at night. I should have known, merely by looking at your face, that you couldn't be . . . evil. And now I've shown that *I* . . . I am too foul to be a good man's companion.'' She shivered. ''Perhaps you're thinking you shouldn't have saved me.''

''No. I can't blame you for the deeds you were forced to commit. One's own survival, after all, is always most important.'' He laughed a dry, humorless laugh. ''How well I know it.''

''Then you don't . . . loathe me?''

''I think perhaps you loathe yourself enough for two.''

Her voice caught in a sob. ''I will cook your meals and mend your clothes and warm your bed—''

''Mizella, I rescued you because you were there, because you were a human being in danger, and because in recent times I have learned to be a little less selfish than I once was. I don't want you to think there was anything else involved.''

''I know,'' she whispered. ''You don't love me. I don't expect it, not the kind of love you reserve for *her*. But that doesn't mean we can't be together. Ah, minstrel, don't drive me away; I won't try to replace her in your heart. You once said I was attractive. . . . Have you changed your mind so soon?''

''No.''

''Then what is the difference between lying with me in the loft and lying with me in the forest or beyond?''

He glanced at her, saw only sparkling eyes in a shadowy face. She seemed very small and vulnerable at that moment, and he felt a surge of responsibility— almost guilt—for having removed her unasked from the life she knew, ugly though it was. He clutched at that responsibility, grateful for its existence, and held it firmly between himself and the past. "No difference at all," he said. "Stay with me, then, and we'll see how well we travel together."

Her step was lighter now. "Perhaps along the way, you could teach me something about being a witch."

He shook his head. "I don't know how. I think I must have been born a witch; I've had this special ability as long as I can remember."

"How did you first discover it?"

He poured out his story, then, and she walked close to his side, clinging to his arm. Not Solinde, not the girl his thoughts constantly turned to, but someone to keep the lonely wind away.

The Witch
and the Well

Moonlight, Alaric thought, stripped ten years from Mizella's life; it blurred the crow's-feet at the corners of her eyes and softened the rough, red skin of her hands as well as any lotion. By moonlight she stirred a pot of stew and added twigs to the fire beneath it, humming tunelessly all the while.

Alaric plucked at his lute with unconscious skill, drawing from it an aimless, melancholy air to fit his melancholy thoughts. Just before sunset, he had climbed a thick-boled oak and, hanging high in the air amid the waxy, dark-green leaves of summer, he scanned the horizon and finally sighted a village of some hundred houses among the low hills to the north. It was the very first sign of human life—barring a weather-beaten farmhouse that sheltered only a family of foxes—that they had encountered since leaving the perpetual twilight of the great forest. A village meant copper and silver, fresh-baked bread, a mattress of straw instead of twigs, and a roof to ward off the elements and the morning dew, yet the young minstrel felt no elation in himself, no pleasure at the prospect of meeting other human beings. That one other human being for whom he cared would not be there—he had only the memory of her, and a favor of black silk fancifully embroidered, that could not fill the emptiness of his heart.

He glanced up at Mizella, who was warm and willing flesh and blood. She was crushing fragrant herbs
between the thumb and forefinger of her right hand,
strewing the powder over their bubbling dinner.

"We'll have no trouble reaching the village tomorrow," he said.

She smiled. "You must be tired of such a small
audience as I."

"Not so tired, but at least I won't have to procure
our meals from old Trif any more."

"The misbegotten scum," she muttered, her mood
shifting abruptly. "You and I worked long enough for
those few provisions; he owes us more than a pair of
chickens or a slab of mutton."

"I won't argue with that, but I'll be pleased to avoid
such danger in the future and earn our fare in a less
exciting manner."

"There is no danger for you," she said firmly.

His fingers struck a discord. "You are far more certain of that than I."

"What has a witch to fear?"

"A real witch, who could summon a spirit to his
aid or form an invisible barrier about his body with
the wave of a hand, would have nothing at all to fear.
But real witches do not exist, else they'd rule the world
and folk would not merely *believe* in them but would
know, without doubt. I am not a real witch, no matter
what you say, Mizella, and I can die as easily as any
man. I dodge a bit faster, nothing else."

Mizella lifted a skeptical eyebrow. "Trif knows you
can't be killed."

"I've been lucky. But I have only one pair of eyes.
If Trif and the others weren't cowards who dare slay
only sleeping men, they would post a guard in the
kitchen. I fear that, Mizella. If I keep returning to the
inn, they will either desert the place from fear or gather

up the courage to wait for me with naked swords. One or the other. They won't be able to bear my visits much longer. I've had enough of them; I won't go back again.''

''Not even for Trif's gold?''

''No. Least of all for that, for he keeps it in his bedchamber. I'm not greedy enough to take that chance.''

''I wish I could have seen his face the moment after we vanished into thin air,'' said Mizella. She stirred the stew so vigorously that it slopped over, making the fire hiss and crackle. ''I wonder if he fell on his knees and cried out to the Holy Ones, begging forgiveness for his evil deeds. Perhaps even now he lives in terror of your return, not to steal a bit of meat from the kitchen but to steal the heart and liver from his body.'' She turned angry eyes to her companion. ''I wish you would kill him!''

Alaric grimaced and glanced away. He didn't like to see Mizella this way, commanding him to be an avenging demon. Trif and his henchmen were murderers, but Alaric had no desire to be the hand of justice. Mizella bore on her back the marks of Trif's whip, and Alaric himself could not forget the clash of steel on sharp-honed steel and the red glare of death in Trif's eyes. But he was glad to be gone and free and alive, and if his hunting skills had been as polished as his musical ones he would never have gone back to the Inn of the Black Swan beyond reclaiming his horse and his lute deep in the night.

''Mizella, you hate too hard,'' he said.

''And you don't hate hard enough. If I had your power . . . if *I* had your power, what vengeance I would wreak on some who deserve all I could give and more! If only you could teach me. . . ?''

''No. There is nothing to be taught.'' He turned his

back on her, to cut off the oft-repeated question and
to gather a few more parched sticks for the fire. He
had known hate a time or two—the stepfather whose
resentment drew an echo from a small boy's soul; the
unknown, unseen bandits who had cut short a beloved
life; the King whose word had banished him from the
sight of the face that haunted his dreams. Yes, he had
known hate and, worse, self-hate: for loving the un-
attainable and nearly destroying it; for running craven
when a better man would have stood and faced his
fate. But hate was an emotion too violent for a young
minstrel's heart to nourish forever: it had faded in
weeks or months or years. He hoped that it would do
the same for her.

"Mizella, I have been thinking," he said. "You've
lived in the land of Durman, have you not?"

"Yes, some years, mostly in the city of Majinak."

"Are your children there?"

"My children. . . ?" She glanced up sharply. "Why
do you ask?"

He thrust a twig into the fire. "I thought, if you
wanted to find them—"

"No!" Her fingers tightened on the stirring spoon.
"No," she said, her voice more controlled. "I'm
sure they are happier where they are, wherever they
are. They wouldn't want a whore for a mother, not a
whore who abandoned them because they threatened
her livelihood. Would you want to meet such a mother?"

"Well . . . yes. I would like to meet my mother.
I would like to know the color of her hair, her eyes,
and whether she is rich or poor. I have often wondered about her and wondered why she left me to
die. Perhaps her reasons were the same as yours.
Perhaps I am a whore's bastard. But I would like to
know."

"She's glad you can't find her to ask."

"*You* are glad, on *your* children's account."

"Yes."

"I'm sorry."

She sighed, and her voice fell soft and hesitant. "I see them in my dreams sometimes: the girl is dark and small, like me, and her face is my face when I was young; the boy is a blurred stranger—I think I would know him if only I could see his features clearly. Let's speak of something else."

"Let's speak of dinner."

"It's ready." She ladled the steaming stew onto their tin plates, and they ate in silence. Later, he sang a little, and she listened.

The village was the hub of a system of fields that sprawled in irregular quadrilaterals over the hilly countryside. Shortly past dawn, whole families were working these tracts—bent-backed oldsters, young women in dun-colored dresses, and scrambling, half-clad children weeded and hoed among the barley and beans. A herd of black cattle, kept from the grain by whistling, shouting, barelegged youths and yelping dogs, cropped the grass that grew knee-high in fallow patches. The dogs were first to take note of Alaric and Mizella, and they approached with caution, alternately barking and growling.

"Hullo!" Alaric shouted to no one in particular and to anyone within earshot. He waved toward the nearest cluster of toilers.

Heads came up and eyes squinted at the two strangers who rode a single gray horse. Pitchforks and scythes appeared, previously hidden by the tall grass and the taller grain. A woman, heavy in the last weeks of pregnancy, backed away; three men moved to shield her as they advanced.

These folk have seen bandits lately, Alaric thought, and he smiled till his cheeks ached.

"Who would you be?" asked the nearest man. He brandished a pitchfork. Sweat gleamed on his bare shoulders and dampened his sunbleached hair, though the day was not yet hot.

Alaric dismounted, leaving Mizella in the saddle. He was virtually unarmed, the sword he scarcely knew how to use well-wrapped in his bedroll, the dagger sheathed at his waist. "I am Alaric the minstrel, and this is the lady Mizella. Weary of travel, we seek shelter and offer a song in return.

"You come from the south."

"No," said Alaric, guessing from the sharp tone of voice that marauders had swooped down upon the village from that direction. "From the east, good sir. We turned north only after spying your homes from afar and yearning for the comforts they represented."

Mizella strummed the lute, which she had carried under one arm since they left their campsite.

The farmers had banded together now, a phalanx bristling with steel points. They were unwashed, sweaty men, muscular, most naked to the waist. Behind them, the young cowherds clutched stout staves, and the smallest children hid among the peacefully grazing cattle. The women were already halfway to the village, walking backwards to keep watch on the confrontation.

With a broad gesture, Alaric reached for the lute, drew it from Mizella's hands, and plucked the lowest string. He sang of the beautiful witch whose garden grew nothing but weeds because a flock of birds ate all the herb and flower seeds: robins, thrushes, and jays—all were suitors who had wished to end her solitary days, enchanted by her own hand and meting out the only retribution within their power, At last, she lifted the enchantments, and marjoram, basil, and thyme, purple larkspur and pink cowslips flourished once more about her cottage, and the young men—wiser and warier—found themselves plain unmagical brides. But the song had a sad ending: many years later, when the witch began at last to feel the loneliness of her life, there was no one to ask for her hand; all were fearful of enchantment, for the tale had spread far and wide. And so she died alone, and the melody ceased with a mournful wail.

The farmers whispered among themselves, and at last their spokesman said, "We see you are indeed a minstrel, but as to whether you may stay in our village, that is a matter for Harbet to decide."

"I will sing for Lord Harbet, then."

"He is no lord, merely a peasant like the rest of us, but he is wise in the ways of the land and of men. Follow me."

Alaric remounted behind Mizella and followed. Most of the other farmers fell in at his left and right, their heads and pitchforks cocked in his direction.

"I don't like this," said Mizella. "Why don't we just pass this village by?"

Alaric shrugged. "I've seen this kind of treatment before, where the arm of the King or the Count or the Duke is weak and the people have to guard themselves. These suspicions pass after a few songs."

"Oh, innocent minstrel! Have you forgotten the Inn of the Black Swan so soon?"

"A whole village? Well, we will keep our eyes open, but I think they fear we are bandits, rather than being such themselves." He stroked her arm reassuringly.

The narrow, crooked pathway that entered the town

was rutted from the wheels of many carts and littered with the dung of many cows; it steamed in the early morning sun. Houses, painted red and black and white with symbols intended to ward off evil, huddled together within the village walls, each separated from its neighbor by a space only wide enough for a tiny garden of turnips or carrots or berries. In the center of the settlement, facing a sizable open space containing a well, was the home of the headman; larger than all the rest, it boasted two windows, one on either side of the extra-broad doorway. Both sets of shutters were partly open to the mild summer air, and red homespun curtains rippled within.

The leader of the farmers leaned in one of the windows and shouted, "Harbet!"

Harbet opened the door. He was a huge man, his shoulders wide and muscular, his beard black as pitch, his skin deeply bronzed. He bore a cudgel in one fist and a huge hammer in the other. "Who calls Harbet?" he roared, his voice a bass drum roll.

The reply was so low-pitched that Alaric could not hear it above the wind and the buzzing conversation of the other villagers around him. He smiled again to all of them, and he dismounted to doff his cap and bow to the man in authority.

"Minstrel, minstrel," said Harbet at last. "Well, I suppose I must let you lie in my house this night, but I'll not stand a second! Someone else must take you if you stay beyond tomorrow."

Alaric shrugged. "We stay as long as a song is welcome."

The man who had called at the window raised his arm. "My house has room enough."

"So be it," Harbet replied.

Alaric reached up to help Mizella slide from the saddle. "We thank you, gentles," he said. "And now, if someone will see to my horse, and if someone else will bring a pair of stools, we will sit here in the square where any may listen.''

''Not in the square!'' said Harbet, and a sudden murmur from the crowd underlined his words. He cleared his throat. ''We are hardworking folk; we have no time to sit in the sun and listen to a minstrel pass the hours. Our fields require attention, our herds require attention. Later, when the candles must be lit and each man may relax after his dinner—*then* we may listen. And until then, minstrel, I suggest that you come inside, drink a cup of wine, and watch my wife spin.''

Alaric glanced about, saw the villagers nodding agreement; several turned immediately and hurried up the street.

''Come in,'' said Harbet. ''There's carrot bread as well as wine, and my wife won't mind a song to speed the thread.''

The interior of the house—one great room—was colorful and cluttered. The double bed in the far corner, the smaller bed nearby, the table and six stools—all were painted with magical devices; elaborate characters were even incised into the hard wood of the table-top, where scraps of food and fragments of wool had stuck in the grooves. Charms hung on the walls, and onions at the windows, and the woman who spun gray wool by the fire wore a sprig of willow in her hair, proof against the evil eye. Alaric had never before seen so much evidence of superstition in one place.

Their host measured the wine carefully and the bread less so. After serving his guests and taking a generous portion for himself, he introduced his wife, Zinovev.

''I know a song about her—the original Zinovev,''

Alaric said. "Legend says she was a lovely lady, even
as you are, my lady."

She blushed and smiled with downcast eyes and
pumped the treadle of the spinning wheel a little
harder. The compliment was fantasy, for she was plain
and freckled and thin to emaciation, and there were
dark circles under her eyes from too much late work.
But she dressed neatly, though in plain homespun, and
her hair was combed and fastened with a fillet—
she cared about her appearance, as a headman's
wife should, and in this she was far lovelier than
many a pretty slattern Alaric had met in his wanderings.

"Zinovev," he said, "was mistress to a great lord
who ruled near the Eastern Sea. He gave her a palace,
jewels, furs, everything a woman could desire, and
when he fell on low times, she was his strong right
arm." He sang of her childhood as the youngest
daughter of an impoverished house, of her early marriage to an old man, of his death and her subsequent
pilgrimage to the Holy Well at Canby, of her meeting
with the great lord, who was disguised and must remain nameless for the sake of the singer's life. He sang
of her palace, set on an island offshore and, by chance
rather than intention, an impregnable fortification;
there, when he was defeated a dozen times over in
battle, came her lord, desiring only to bid her a last
farewell and throw himself from the highest parapet of
a tower that overhung the sea. But Zinovev convinced
him to raise a fresh army and try once more to recap-
ture his lost lands; together they planned his cam-
paigns, directing them from horseback or from tents
on the windswept northern plains or from shipboard
near the coast, and at last they regained his power,
and a peace settled on his domain. He offered Zinovev
anything, everything, but she wanted only his happi-

ness and was content with her island palace and his love. Which, of course,'' said Alaric, when the song was done, ''meant that she did indeed have everything, for what man can deny the woman who holds his heart?''

''How beautiful,'' murmured Harbet's wife. ''I did not know there was such a famous Zinovev. My mother heard the name once and loved it.'' She glanced at her husband. ''What a fine voice the young man has.''

Harbet shrugged. ''I have work to finish.'' He walked out and closed the door hard behind him.

Zinovev rose from her spinning. ''Please forgive my husband for his rudeness; as headman, he must host every traveler who passes this way. And not many months ago, we were attacked by bandits—they looted and burned three houses at the south edge of the village before we were able to drive them off, and the homeless families had to stay with us, of course, until their new houses were built. The crowding, the eating of a good deal of our substance, made his temper short. Please, have some more wine, we have plenty.''

Alaric accepted a second cup. ''Forgive me for saying this, but if he doesn't like being headman. . . .''

''His grandfather's grandfather founded this village,'' she replied, ''and the headmanship stayed in the family; our fellow-villagers would have it no other way. My eldest son will take it next.'' She pulled the full spindle from the spinning wheel, dropped it into a large black kettle on the floor. ''He likes it, but he would never tell anyone that. It's just his way.''

''I see.''

''I for one am glad to be a headman's wife, for we are first host to travelers who bring news of the world. Have you come from Eliath, perhaps, or Berentil?''

Alaric shook his head. ''From the east, from Castle Royale and farther. We wander forever and have no home. Would you care for news of the east?''

She sat at the table and ate a few crumbs of carrot bread. ''The east? There is nothing in the east but the forest which stretches to the end of the world.''

''And the folk in the east think there is nothing in the west but the forest which stretches to the end of the world. Well, some few of them know of Durman. Is this village part of Durman?''

''Yes, though the very edge.''

At that moment, the door burst open, slamming back against the wall, and four dirty youngsters filled the room, laughing and chattering, screaming and crying and clattering.

''What's this, what's this?'' said Zinovev as the smallest flung himself into her arms, wailing.

''He hit me, he hit me!'' he sobbed, pointing vaguely toward the others.

Zinovev stroked his head, holding him close. She looked up at the others and pointed imperiously to the floor in front of her feet. They lined up like soldiers at inspection and were immediately silent.

''What happened?''

The tallest boy replied, ''Papa said come in for lunch and Pegwy didn't want to, so I hit him.''

''Pegwy,'' she said, holding the sobbing boy at arm's length, ''is that true?''

''I was blowing on the fire, Mama. I would have been done soon.'' He was a tiny fellow, no more than six years old, and his pale hair was streaked with soot.

''It was not necessary to hit him, Garet. Next time, let him finish what he is doing. Understood?''

Garet frowned. "Sometimes he never finishes."

"Then tell me and I will call him. I don't want the headman's children fighting in front of the whole village."

"We were in the smithy."

"And I don't want you hitting your little brother. Not until he's big enough to fight back properly. Now, go get some water and clean yourselves; we have guests for the day."

The children looked around, noticing Alaric and Mizella for the first time. They smiled with sudden shyness, and then they ran out, four barefoot, towheaded boys. Alaric watched them through the window as they crossed the square—two had picked up buckets outside the door, but instead of going to the well, they gave it a wide berth and disappeared among the houses on the far side.

"Handsome children," he said truthfully.

"Dirty children," said Zinovev, "but you shall see them in better condition shortly."

"They're going to wash?"

"Yes."

"They passed the well."

"The well is dry. They'll go to the spring on the other side of the hill."

He squinted at the well—the neatly mortared stones had been daubed with the same magical patterns as every house in the village. The colors were bright, unweathered, recent. He wondered if they thought evil spirits had driven off the water.

While the children ate and prattled, Alaric sat in the corner with Mizella, tuning the lute. "Is all Durman so full of superstition?" he whispered.

"Charms, amulets, talismans, I have seen, but *this* . . . this is beyond the ordinary. Unless . . . unless they have had some experience of witchcraft.

And recently, for the paint is no more than a year old.''

"They might paint over the same patterns every year.''

"You think this village is rich enough to purchase paint every year?''

"I suppose not. The bandits may have something to do with it. Might they think the bandits were brought by witchcraft?''

"I've never heard of that. Bandits come with no aid from the Dark One, save moral support. But the well is dry.''

"Yes, the well is dry. But wells dry up by themselves.''

"Perhaps . . . but perhaps,'' she murmured in the lowest possible voice, "you have a brother witch in this village.''

Alaric frowned. "I can't make a well go dry.''

"Another kind of witch, then?''

"There is no other kind of witch.''

Mizella pursed her lips. "Many people would disagree with you. I remember a witch who was drowned in Majinak; she caused the lord's horse to throw him— broke his neck.''

"Coincidence.''

"The lord's son thought not.''

"He was wrong. In Castle Royale, where I once lived for a time, they burned supposed witches—old women whose only crime was ugliness. It would seem that people always wish to blame their misfortune on *someone* rather than on chance or perhaps their own stupidity.''

"Yet you sing of witches.''

"My songs are pure invention. Anything can happen in a song.''

Mizella sighed. "Ah, minstrel, you are young to be so certain."

"Very young," he said, nodding, "but my master was also certain, and I have seen no evidence to shake that certainty. Come, let's join our hostess and her family."

The children were finishing the last crumbs of their carrot bread, the last drops of their milk. They turned clean faces to the minstrel and smiled.

"My sweet ones," said Zinovev, "your father is surely ready for your return."

They stretched and yawned in chorus and giggled at each other before pushing back their stools and rushing out as they had first rushed in. The youngest, little Pegwy, was last; his tears were gone now. He glanced back as he crossed the threshold, and he waved to Alaric.

"He loves a new face," said his mother. "He'll be on your lap if you don't take care."

Alaric watched them cross in front of the window, and the well beyond them caught his gaze and held it long after the children were gone. He noticed now that it was sealed with a carefully made round lid of planks.

"They all work in the smithy with their father—dirty work, but honest," Zinovev said. She cleared the crumbs from the table with a flick of her hand. "The eldest has already made a dozen tools, and the next is not far behind. Others in the village have asked Harbet to apprentice their younger sons, but he felt that his own should come first. Minstrel?"

"Yes?"

"Minstrel, you must not stare at the well like that."

"If you wish me not to stare, good lady, I will not

stare. But I was noticing the intricacy of design, the delicate execution of the strokes—''

''It is an unlucky well, minstrel.'' Her hands fluttered about the mantel for a moment, and then she found a fresh spindle and resumed her place at the wheel. ''This has been an unlucky year for us—the bandits, the dry well, the poor weather, a low yield of crops, and other things. . . . We are hoping for the best, we are fighting evil as well as we can—you can understand our desire to think only of the good, can't you?''

''Of course, my lady.''

''The well . . . we don't look at it, we don't speak of it, we stay away from it. Some evil spirit has been in our village, and we are battling the Dark One with everything we have.'' She glanced up at the nearest charm, she touched the willow twig in her hair. ''We pray that next year will be a better one.''

''I fervently hope it will be, my lady, and I beg forgiveness for causing you any discomfort.''

''No, no, it's all right. It's my husband that is most distressed. I warn you in advance.''

''And I thank you for the warning.''

''You are most welcome, minstrel.'' She looked up, met his eyes with her own, and smiled slowly. ''Most welcome.''

''Alaric,'' said Mizella, laying her hand on his arm, ''will you sing another song?''

He obliged but hardly knew what he sang—something about a butterfly. He read with ease the emotions that flickered across Mizella's face. Envy: their hostess was no more than a year or two older and she appeared to be exactly the sort of person Mizella wished to be—wife to an important man, mother of fine children, comfortable and respected. Jealousy: this fine, clean woman, who surely had no crimes on her conscience, had cast her eyes on Alaric, and Alaric had read the message in those eyes often enough before to recognize it. He was young and slim and straight, he was a wanderer from far away and a minstrel; Dall had often told him that there was something about minstrels that women invariably loved, and Alaric had learned the truth of that in recent years. He had read the message aright, but he had not and would not acknowledge it—not the headman's wife. He was young, but he was not stupid.

Mizella borrowed a needle and thread and repaired a rip in her gown. Alaric carved a new lute peg to replace one which was cracked. Zinovev spun and spun. The afternoon passed, and evening came on. At sunset, Harbet and the children closed the smithy and came in for a brief supper of cold smoked meat and boiled turnips. Zinovev had hardly cleared the table when the villagers started to arrive.

One after another, they crowded in the door, filling the house, pushing aside the table, sitting on the stools and the bed and the floor, craning over each other's shoulders for a good view of the minstrel. Women came, dressed in their best dark floor-sweeping gowns and dark shawls, their hair wound in braids about their heads and decorated with willow leaves. Men came, wearing embroidered vests of red and green and yellow, carrying lavishly carved hardwood walking sticks. Children entered, clinging to their mothers' hands or walking boldly behind their fathers—children in ribbons and laces, with shiny metal buckles on their shoes. They came and filled the house to bursting, and fathers raised their small sons on their shoulders, so high that wet, well-combed heads brushed the low ceiling.

Alaric backed into the corner by the spinning wheel.

"I've rarely attracted so eager an audience," he told his host.

"Mind you, don't stand on the bed!" Harbet shouted. "That bed was never meant for the weight of so many!" He swore under his breath.

"Surely we would be more comfortable outside," said Alaric. "Even with the windows and the door open, this room will soon be overwarm from many bodies."

Harbet glared at the minstrel. "Not outside," he said.

"I'm not accustomed to singing in such close quarters."

"No? Then some must go home. And scarcely a third of the village is here tonight." He turned to make the announcement.

Alaric touched his arm. "Let it be. I would not turn away such eager music lovers." He grinned. "But I will stand by the window, for I would not be the first to swoon." With the aid of his host, he elbowed his way through the crowd and settled himself on a stool in the path of the cool night breeze. Already, several in the audience were sweating.

"What sort of song shall it be, good sir?" he said to Harbet. "A tale of woe or a rhyme to laugh at? Dragons and gnomes and high sorcery, or sword-swinging knight and fair princess?"

"I don't care," said Harbet.

"The knight!" cried the headman's youngest boy.

"The knight it shall be." And he obliged with an epic well-known in his previous haunts but which he hoped would prove a novelty to the folk of Durman: the song of Kilaran, who yearned to be the best knight in the world and spent his life meeting every test that men and demons could devise. Wounded, he fought the seven-handed monster of Slathrum and left it bloody and dying in the forest; armed only with a song, he won the most beautiful woman in the world for his wife. "And let that demonstrate the power of music," Alaric said, ending the story with an extended chord.

"I would liefer believe in the power of music if he had beaten the bandits and the monsters with its aid," said Harbet.

"I have one of those, too," said Alaric, and he launched into the tale of the man who knew the secret magical songs that brought him everything his heart desired, until he grew bored with that life and cut out his tongue to rid himself of magic forever.

Toward the end of this song, Alaric heard a noise like a dog howling, far off, indistinct, but plaintive. He fancied he could almost hear words in the howl, though he could make out no meaning, and he felt pity for the poor creature. He wondered if its masters were all at his performance and had left it tied up alone in the dark outside their house. A few people in the audience seemed to notice the sound, glancing toward the windows and the door and each other, but no one made any move to alleviate the creature's suffering.

When he finished his tragic story, the minstrel said, "Is that a dog?"

There were a few murmurs from his listeners, but no clear answer.

"The wind," said Harbet.

Alaric listened carefully for a moment. "It doesn't sound like the wind to me. Perhaps something is wrong. . . ."

"It's nothing," said Harbet. "Sing again."

Alaric glanced around, sensing an uneasiness in the audience. Women were shifting in their seats, gathering their children a trifle closer; men slipped their arms about their wives' shoulders. Many—the major-

ity of the adults—looked to Harbet anxiously, but he
gave no special sign. He gazed sidewise toward Zinovev, who had drawn her two younger sons tight to her
bosom.

"Sing again," Harbet commanded. "We give you
hospitality in return for songs!"

Alaric strummed a chord and tried a happy tune, a
tale of gossiping women who turned a whole town upside down with unfounded rumors of the King's visit.
Each stanza portrayed some townsman in an amusing
situation as a result of his haste to prepare for the royal
visit; Alaric had often known listeners to laugh at this
song till their faces went crimson, but tonight there
were only a few giggles from the youngsters in the
crowd and a nervous smile or two from their elders,
nothing more.

"Enough," said Harbet at last. "We rise early."
He motioned toward the door, and the villagers fairly
scrambled to leave, parents gripping their children by
hand or arm or shoulder with stiff, white-knuckled fingers. They poured into the square, recoiled from the
well, and crossed to their homes by hugging the cot-
tages at the edge of the open space. They were quickly
gone, flowing through the gaps between buildings like
water through the mesh of a sieve, and the sound of
many doors slamming, of many bolts being shot home,
echoed over the hills.

Harbet slammed his own door and shot its bolt,
swung the shutters in and latched them also, and then
he touched the coin that hung from a thong at his neck,
and his ragged breathing calmed.

"You'll sleep on the children's cot," he said to Alaric, gesturing toward the larger of the two beds.

"No," said Zinovev. She stood in the far corner,
behind the spinning wheel, her arms encircling all her
sons. Her eyes were wide, and there was fear in them.

"They will sleep in *our* bed, and I shall sleep with the children in theirs."

Harbet crossed his arms over his massive chest. "And where will *I* sleep?"

"At the door."

"At the door?"

"Yes. Guarding your family from all evil."

"This family is guarded well enough by that and that and that!" He pointed to the paint, the carvings, the trinkets hung on the walls.

The howling commenced once more, louder this time, and now Alaric was certain that he could make out words in that desolate cry. "Surely that is some human being wailing for aid!" he said, and he reached for the shutter latch, intending to throw the window open and look out.

Harbet stopped him with an iron hand on his shoulder. "We don't open them again once they're shut for the night."

"But someone is suffering out there!"

"I pray so," said Harbet.

"Husband, I can't bear it much longer!" Zinovev cried wildly, her hands clapped over her ears.

"Would you have me leave this village?" Harbet shouted.

She turned to the wall. "Perhaps it would be better."

"This is *my* village, *my* people, and I won't leave them, do you hear me? I will never leave them! Let her howl every night! We will go on in spite of her! Oh, the evil day—the evil day that ever we welcomed her!"

"Yes, yes, but lamenting the evil day resolves nothing!"

"Silence, woman! No more of this before our guests!"

"You will sleep at the door."

Harbet swore through clenched teeth. "Very well. I will sleep at the door. I will sleep on willow at the door."

Zinovev knelt by the larger of the two beds and dragged from beneath it a bulky comforter—an excessive stiffness and the many sharp points poking at the cloth surface from within betrayed a stuffing of twigs. She laid this pallet at the threshold and threw a light woolen coverlet over it. "Good night."

The howling ceased abruptly.

"You see," he said. "The very presence of willow at the door discourages her."

"Then we will keep it there every night." She herded the children into bed, banked the fire for the night, and blew out the candles that had been lit at sunset, leaving the room dim and red.

"Good sir," Alaric ventured, "who is that you fear so greatly?"

"He who asks no questions learns no sorrow, minstrel," said Harbet. Dry twigs snapped loudly beneath his weight.

"I see," said Alaric. He lay back on his cot.

Mizella clung close. "We can't stay here," she whispered. "These people are mad or bewitched!"

A few feet away, the children giggled softly at some private joke.

"Neither," he replied. "Merely frightened, apparently of some madwoman who wanders about at night and howls." In the darkness, he could barely discern the silhouette of Zinovev as she undressed.

"May we leave in the morning?"

"Do you wish to travel on so quickly? To where?"

"Anywhere. Their fear suffocates me."

"There is nothing to be afraid of, and I would like to relax a few days and eat a stranger's food. Who knows what lies down the road? Let us take advantage of what we have here."

"Youth makes you fearless . . . and foolish."

"My fears require metal armor, not paint. Someday I will win you to my view, Mizella, and you will be happier knowing the world is empty of dark powers beyond the control of man."

"I am happy . . . and fearless with you, my lord." She kissed his neck and laid her head comfortably on his shoulder for sleep.

Am I the only one, Alaric wondered, *the only one who disbelieves now that Dall is dead?*

He slept and dreamed of formless shadows arching over him. But he dispelled them with a word: Solinde—and her pale face filled his world with light.

He woke to Mizella's touch. "Good morning, dear minstrel."

The door and windows were open, and Harbet's family was already at the table for a breakfast of barley porridge.

"Truly, I would like to sit outside in the sunlight," Alaric told his host.

Harbet scowled, "Well, if you must, come round to the smithy and sing to the beat of the hammer."

"I'll do that."

Zinovev smiled, and the children smiled, and it seemed to Alaric that last night must have been merely an extension of his dream. But the charms and carvings and carefully executed magical symbols on the well assured him otherwise.

The smithy was a separate building with its own roaring fire and tall chimney; the implements of Harbet's trade hung on a wooden rack above the anvil, and a pile of iron bars waited on the bench to be forged into tools.

"While Papa builds up the fire, sing another song about knights, please, minstrel," said Pegwy, who had carried out a pair of stools for Alaric and Mizella. "I did so love the one last night!"

"You work the bellows, don't you?"

"Yes, but not at the beginning. Please, minstrel?"

Alaric sat just beyond the shade of the smithy roof and sang about knights and dragons and fair maidens. Villagers on their way to the fields stopped a moment to listen, women stood in their doorways or leaned on their windowsills to listen before beginning the day's labor indoors. Children carrying twin buckets of water strung from neck yokes paused on their way home from the spring and gazed with envious eyes at the headman's sons.

"You can stay with us tomorrow, minstrel!" called a plump, red-faced woman in a blue dress and cap. She waved from her doorway. "I have a fresh-baked fowl, and honey for your tea!"

"I have veal stew!" cried another woman.

"And I have apple pie and strawberries!" offered a third.

Alaric bowed to each of them. "Thank you, good ladies. You make us feel welcome in your village." He leaned over to Mizella and muttered, "I suppose we're too far from civilization to expect hard money."

To listen to the song, Pegwy had sat down cross-legged on the hard-packed earth at Alaric's feet; now he jumped up at his father's summons. "I must work now, minstrel, and I won't be able to hear you above the sounds of the fire and the hammer, but will you sing another for me later? Another about knights and swords and horses?"

Alaric smiled and ruffled the boy's blond hair. "If you like, youngster."

"Oh, thank you, thank you, minstrel!" His grin seemed likely to burst his cheeks. "I hope you stay here a long time!" He skipped into the smithy and took up his place at the fire, where he pumped the bellows with a steady, even hand. His father laid a bar in the flames, waited till it turned red hot, then took it out and hammered, shedding a million red sparks over the anvil. Pegwy watched, learning his future trade, and he worked the bellows smoothly all the while.

"Hard labor," said Mizella.

"But profitable," Alaric returned. "When he grows up, he'll earn more in a day than I do in a month."

"Not here. In a city like Majinak perhaps, but not here."

"He'll be comfortable. I've never yet heard of a smith who starved. And he'll dream . . . of being a knight. The ones who love those songs . . . Dall told me that they always dreamed of being knights."

"You never dreamed of being a knight?"

"Not I. I've had a taste of the training involved—a minstrel's life promotes fewer sore muscles. One lives longer this way, too, and makes fewer enemies."

"Ah, yes. Dear minstrel, you must have no enemies at all."

He shrugged. He'd never told her that he was exiled from Castle Royale for seducing the King's daughter. There was one enemy at least: the King himself; and the court magician also had little love for Alaric. Far behind, two enemies. And equally far behind, the young heir to the throne and the big-headed, bantering dwarf—friends who saved a foolish minstrel's life. And Solinde . . . Solinde . . . her smile as warm as midday sunlight. . . .

"I brought your luncheon for you," Pegwy said, startling the minstrel from his reverie. He bore two bread trenchers and a couple of chunks of cheese.

Alaric glanced up at the sky. "Is the sun so high already?"

"It's a little early," the child confessed, "but I thought if you ate now, you could play while I have *my* meal. Please?"

"Very well."

Pegwy ran back to the smithy and took up his task once more.

"I think I could make a minstrel of that boy," Alaric murmured.

"Children love music," said Mizella.

"Beyond that, this one has an interest . . . the same interest that led my master to take me on. I was older by a few years, but Pegwy is equally fascinated. See how he glances this way every few moments, as if to assure himself that we are still here? He would learn, I think. I wonder if he can sing."

"Have you need of an apprentice?"

"Need?" He nibbled at the cheese. "No minstrel has need till his voice begins to quaver with age—then he requires an apprentice to earn his bread for him. No, Dall had no need when he taught me, but he knew a loneliness that only another voice could lighten. One voice, he told me, could never sing harmony to itself."

"I'm sorry I can't sing, Alaric."

He leaned over to squeeze her arm. "Dall was far older than I am now; I still have too much pride to let another share the audience's attention with me. If I were . . . say . . . twice my present age, I might think of taking the boy, but not now. I hope I meet another like him *then.*"

"His parents would scarcely allow it anyway," Mizella said, nodding toward the smithy, where Harbet hammered till sweat glistened all over his naked torso.

Alaric examined her face intently, calculated the direction of her gaze. "You want him, don't you? You want him for a son."

"He's a pretty child."

"A bit old to be *my* son."

"Just the right age to be mine." She sighed. "I wish you could give me a son, dear minstrel, or a daughter. I wish someone could give me a babe."

He put his arms around her and held her close, petting her hair.

"I'm sorry," she whispered. "You're too young to be bothered about such things. Never mind, never mind."

"The reason—the ultimate reason why I would not even ask his parents is that . . . the fewer who know about me, the better." He tilted her face up and kissed her lips. "Consider me your child," he said with a grin.

"I do."

"Incestuous wench."

"It's true, sometimes. Sometimes you are my son and sometimes my father. The way you speak and act—you're a strange mixture of old and young."

"That comes of leading the life I've led and knowing the folk I've known. And possessing the talent I possess . . ." He hugged her. "Enough, Mizella, before your flattery turns my head."

"Yes, enough. The sun is bright and hot; perhaps we can move into the shade now? And I think our young friend is waiting for another song."

Pegwy had approached quietly, and now he stretched out on the ground before them. He gobbled his midday meal.

"More knights?" said Alaric, taking up his lute.

Pegwy nodded eagerly, and then he added, "Unless you wish to sing some other kind of song."

"I've a bag full of knights and ten bags full of dragons—they take up so much more space. Once a dragon lived in the great forest, just beyond the smallest, newest village in the whole land. . . ."

Eventually, Pegwy's father called him back to the forge.

"Let's stroll about the village," Alaric suggested, offering his arm to Mizella. She accepted, and they strolled. "I wonder what it is about the well that makes them avoid it so completely." He guided their footsteps toward the square.

"Evil spirits dried it up," Mizella replied.

"Yes, but they've daubed it thoroughly with charms against enchantment—surely it's harmless to them by now, or even beneficial."

She shrugged. "These things take time to fade. On the manor where I grew up, there was a tree blasted by the Dark One, and for years no one would go near it, but eventually the evil wore off and we could pass it without harm."

"Lightning?"

"Of course."

"Then you could have passed it the next day with no harm, as long as the weather was clear. Tall trees attract lightning, like tall towers—the Dark One has nothing to do with it."

"Oh, Alaric, I wish I had your certainty."

Alaric smiled. "Surely if the Dark One existed, *I* would know him." Softly, he hummed the tune that was running through his head, about a white magician who chased the Dark One to his lair demanding concessions, only to inadvertently bind himself to evil. They had approached the well in a long spiral, and now he leaned against it. The square was deserted, and most of the windows facing it were closely shuttered; the few ajar showed darkness within. "You see," he said, "there's nothing to be afraid of."

Abruptly, the howling began, nearer than ever before, and the words were plain: "Help me, help me, help me. . . ."

"It's in the well!" gasped Mizella, backing away in shock.

"In the well. . . ." Alaric placed his ear against the boards that covered the opening, and he could clearly hear the words which came from directly below.

"Help me, please help me, please help me. . . ."

"Someone's down the well!" he shouted to the empty square and the shuttered windows. "Someone's down the well!" With his bare hands he tugged at the longest board of the cover, but it was nailed fast with spikes driven deep into mortared stones. "Help, help!" he cried. "Someone's in the well! Mizella, run for help!"

Help came, a dozen hands, and they dragged Alaric away from the well and inside the headman's house.

"Kill him!" a man was screaming. "Kill him before he brings us more ill fortune!"

"Yes, kill him and throw him in with her," said another. "He touched it; we dare not let him live!"

"Wait!" shouted Alaric, and he struggled as they bound him to the bed in which he had slept the previous night. The ropes were coarse and prickly and rasped his skin. "What's going on here!"

They shoved Mizella into a corner and stood before her, their bodies the bars of her prison. She kicked one of them in the kneecap and was rewarded with a slap that knocked her back against the wall.

Harbet stamped into the room. "What is happening

in my house?'' he roared. A dozen men gabbled at him in explanation, then he raised his hand for silence. He glared down at Alaric. "So you're a friend of hers?"

"You treat a guest very poorly, Harbet," Alaric said in a cold, even tone. "Of whom do you think I am a friend?"

"Her. The witch Artuva."

"I don't know her."

"Then what were you doing at the well?"

"I heard a voice crying for help, my host. I tried to give it, as would any normal man. Someone is down the well!"

"We know that."

"Then in the name of all that's good, why don't you rescue the poor unfortunate?"

"It is the witch Artuva. We put her there, and there she'll stay till she rots!"

The full horror of it sickened Alaric. To be shut up in a dark hole in the ground! "What did she do," he gasped, "to merit such punishment?"

"Enough and more than enough. Pretending to be a midwife, she killed my youngest child at birth, and for that, if nothing else, she must die. You'll not save her, minion of the Dark One."

"Me? I'm no one's minion. I'm a minstrel."

"Lies!" shouted Harbet. "I knew when I first laid eyes on you that you were a witch just like her!"

From the corner came Mizella's sobs.

"Don't be frightened, dear lady," Alaric said. "And you who struck her—"

"Throw him in the well!" said the threatened man. "Throw him in the well before he bewitches us!"

"He'll not bewitch us," Harbet muttered. He ripped open the twig-stuffed comforter and strewed dry wood and crushed willow leaves over Alaric's body.

A cry from the doorway startled the gathering. "Oh, Harbet, what have you done?" Zinovev, returned home from a neighborly visit. She ran to the bedside and stopped there, one hand raised to her mouth. "I heard, but I could not believe. Harbet, he is our *guest!*"

"And a fouler guest we have never hosted."

"He was curious about the well, Harbet. Who wouldn't be curious about all this?" With a sweeping gesture she indicated the carvings and paint and willow and onions and the whole village. "This is laughable, Harbet—as laughable as it is mysterious. Let him go, let her out, set her free. She's proved that she's stronger than we are."

"She'll die in the winter. She can't conjure a fur coat out of nothing."

Zinovev touched his arm. "She's conjured food out of nothing for two months."

"Silence, wife! It can't go on forever, else why send for rescue?"

"Rescue? This boy is no rescue. When the Dark One sends a rescue, he'll send fire and flood and pestilence on us all. He'll come in a fiery chariot drawn by snakes and vultures. He'll leave this land barren to punish us, if he does not carry us all off alive to his kingdom. He'll not send a man and a woman with one horse between them!"

"How do you know?"

Zinovev gazed down at Alaric with tears in her eyes. "His voice is so beautiful. The Dark One is ugly and speaks with the voice of the crow and the frog, not with the voice of the lute."

"Bah! He's a pretty boy. I can see *that* well enough."

Zinovev frowned at him. "So you'll murder him. You might as well be in the service of the Dark One yourself."

"He's a witch."

"He's a young man with an understandable curiosity. Oh, Harbet, you're a fool. I won't live with a fool any longer. My mother's village will welcome me, I am sure."

He caught her arm, bent it behind her back, making her wince. "You'll not desert me now, wife. We'll save this village—the destruction of evil will make us blessed."

"Not murder of the innocent!"

He threw her to the floor with a growl. His sons had come to the door, and they watched the proceedings with wide eyes.

"You've made a terrible mistake, Harbet," said Alaric. "Redeem yourself by setting us free."

The headman laughed mirthlessly. "We'll burn them," he said. "We should have burned the old woman, too."

"Drag her out and burn her with them," said one of the crowd.

Harbet eyed the speaker. "You drag her out, Nagwyn."

Nagwyn glanced at the floor, his lips pursed.

"Who else might be willing to bring the witch out of the well? Ledek? Blas?"

The men named looked uncertainly at one another. They shuffled their feet, and the sweat of fear trickled down their faces.

Harbet clenched his fists. "Leave her," he said firmly. "She'll have to summon the Dark One himself and *all* his minions to escape that prison. These two we'll burn, and we'll take their ashes on a pilgrimage to Arnara—for burial where they'll never be able to harm a living soul. And from Arnara, we will bring back to our village a bit of holy soil to protect us all forever." He gazed from man to man. "Is there any better notion?"

"Arnara is far," said Nagwyn.

"Shall I lay the ashes at your doorstep?" Harbet thundered.

"Well, who will go?" Nagwyn muttered sullenly.

"I will go."

Zinovev clutched at his leg. "You'll die on that holy ground!" she screamed. "No murderer could visit Arnara and live! Harbet, please, for the children—"

He shook her free with a kick. "Come, neighbors, we'll pick them up and carry them out to burn, bed and all!"

"Alaric!" wailed Mizella, as two men laid hands on her.

The bed was empty, the ropes limp without their captive.

Harbet gestured reflexively against evil spirits, and before the sign was complete, Alaric had returned, unbound, standing, a sword in his hand. The villagers were frozen, expressions of horror on their faces, hands trembling, half-raised to amulets or mystic embroidery on their clothing. Mizella was frozen, too, but only for an instant; then she turned, wrenched free of her guards, drove her fists into the groin of the man who had struck her, bloodied the nose of his partner, and ducked between them to reach the minstrel. Alaric caught her on the run, lifted her as the villagers broke from their shock, shouted, closed in . . . on nothing.

South of the village, the forest was cool and shady. Mizella leaned against a tree, breathing raggedly. "I will never become accustomed to that mode of travel, but I am very grateful that it exists."

Alaric let the point of his sword drop to the ground. "I wish it hadn't been necessary. If only I had been

able to reason with them. . . . Now Harbet is quite
certain he was right.'' His lips curved into a wry smile.
''And yet, I've always wanted to do something like
that. Only in the last few years have I had the ability,
the control, to accomplish it.''

Mizella looked up, puzzled. ''What do you
mean?''

He touched the tree, ran his hand over the rough
bark. ''Once, as a child—I think I was six years old—
I was leaning against a tree much like this one, about
the same height and size. I decided to travel to another
part of the wood near my foster parents' home. This
was before I ran away. I thought of the place at which
I wished to be, and I was there in an instant—and
beside me was the selfsame tree I had left behind, all
crowded up against another that had not previously
been beside it. I was surprised indeed, and even more
surprised when it fell over and shattered into a million
pieces. It was only the bark of the tree, you see—I had
only taken the bark with me and left the rest behind,
naked and pale. I had power, but only the barest skill
at using it. Imagine what I could have done to another
human being.''

''Your skill has improved with age, though, and with
practice. You rescued me, both of us, from Trif. . . .''

''I wasn't sure I could do that. I wasn't sure I could
take all of you with me. I'd had some bad luck with a
piece of sheeting not long before . . . but I couldn't
leave you there for him.''

Mizella shivered and hugged herself with crossed
arms. ''I'm glad I didn't know. And yet . . . you could
do it wilfully, could you not? You could go back to the
village and tear Harbet's body apart.''

He glanced down at the roots of the tree, touched
one with the tip of his sword. ''I could, but I won't.''

''He was going to kill us!''

"But he didn't kill us. I'll admit he deserves to be punished, and not merely for what he did and tried to do to us; but he has a family to care for, a whole village dependent on him." His lips pursed, whitened for a moment. "I have never drawn human blood with this sword. I am not an executioner."

"I'd kill him." Her cheeks flushed. "If I could, I'd kill the whole lot of them."

"They won't forget you, especially the one you nearly castrated."

"No." She smiled, self-satisfied, an unpleasant sort of smile.

Alaric sighed, his mind and heart shying away from her hate. He pitied the villagers in their ignorance and panic; he had never feared them. "Mizella?" He propped the sword against the tree, then took her hands between his own. "Mizella, I have to go back for the horse . . . and more."

"The lute," she said, nodding. "You left the lute behind, too. It's lying on the stool by the smithy."

"More than the lute." He squeezed her fingers. "I have to get her out of the well."

She looked up into his eyes. "I know. I've known since we heard her voice. You don't believe in witches, and therefore she's just a suffering woman. But Alaric, she's been down in that well for two months! She *must* be a witch!"

"There's another explanation. There has to be."

"Perhaps she has your power and steals her food that way?"

His eyebrows lifted. "Then why is she still in the well?"

"She must have her reasons!"

"Then I'll ask her for them. Tonight."

"They're frightened—they may already be killing her."

"I think not; their very fear will keep them from it. But to make doubly sure, I'll watch till sunset from safety high on the hill."

Dusk. Alaric appeared behind Harbet's house, in full view of the smithy, where he had not dared to go earlier. The stools were gone, as was his lute, probably taken into the headman's house, possibly burned by now as a witch's token; he winced at the loss of Solinde's silken favor, berated himself for leaving it unattended, and vowed to make a thorough search later, after this night's work was done and after the household was soundly asleep. The smithy was barred, quiet. Without disturbing the door, he ducked inside, secured an iron bar, and came out. Stepping lightly, ready to vanish at the slightest noise, he rounded the house.

The square was dark, save for the pale light of a crescent moon. The windows and doors of the villagers' homes were tight shut, and no one was abroad. Softly, Alaric went to the well and, with the bar as a lever, began to pry up the cover.

A tiny sound made him flit to the safety of the shadows between two houses. One of the shutters at a nearby cottage opened slightly, and a small figure climbed out. Alaric guessed it was a child, but he could not discern its precise identity. The figure approached the well, lifted one of the boards, then lowered it. Alaric waited till the child returned through the shutter, then ventured out again.

He tested all of the boards gently; one proved loose at the near end, and he lifted it. "I'm a friend," he whispered into the deeper darkness of the well. "Please trust me and be silent." There was no answer. He pried at the other boards, and they gave with tiny squeaks. He laid the slats carefully on the ground.

"Stand aside, I'm coming down." He felt certain that her thoroughly dark-adapted eyes would perceive his silhouette against the less dark sky. He swung his legs over the side of the well and lowered himself into the abyss. A parched, musty smell assailed his nostrils; the well was indeed dry as dust. Bracing his back against one side of the shaft, his feet against the other, he inched his way downward. At last, a hand touched him.

"This is the bottom, friend." An old, old woman's voice, less a whisper than a croak. "You are the singer, are you not?"

"Yes, good lady."

"I hoped a stranger would have pity. . . . But where is your rope?"

"We've no need of a rope, my good lady. Allow me to put my arms around you, and we shall leave this place in an instant."

"What? You'll carry me up as you came down? Sir, you jest."

For answer, Alaric circled her with his arms and lifted; he found her wispy-light, lighter even than Mizella, and he knew there would be no difficulty.

Mizella had started a fire and gathered handfuls of wild blackberries for their refreshment. By firelight, the lady of the well was shriveled and bent-backed, a tiny woman made tinier by her crouching posture. She blinked at the fire and shielded her eyes with her right hand, in which she clutched a chunk of cold roast meat. Her skin and hair were dirty, encrusted with grime, as were the voluminous rags that formed her clothing.

"I had given up hope," she said, and sank to the ground, shaking with sobs, her eyes shut tight.

Mizella took the old woman in her arms and crooned the words a mother used to comfort an unhappy child.

Alaric went to the barn where Lightfoot was still sta-
bled, found the water flask still hung on his saddle,
and filled it from a brook many miles and days away—
the villagers had spoken of a spring on the far side of
their hill, but Alaric had never seen it and thus could
not travel to the place in his own manner. This other
water source, however, was not far for one such as he.
He had been gone but a few moments when he returned to hand the full container to Mizella, who
soaked a strip of her petticoat and wiped the old woman's face with it.

"Thank you, thank you," whispered the oldster. "I
have had so little water. . . . How long was I down
there?"

"They said two months," Alaric told her. "How
did you manage to survive?" He already had an
inkling of her answer.

"The children, the wonderful children. In the middle of the night they brought me water and food—
crusts and meat scraps and whatever other tidbits they
could steal, but still a feast for a starving woman. The
children . . . and especially little Pegwy, may the Holy
Ones bless him."

Alaric glanced at Mizella. "They never suspected
their own children. They thought that when the doors
and windows were barred for the night that none would
dare venture out."

The woman raised her eyes to him. "Lord, I thank
you for saving me, and I beg to know how I may be
of service to you."

"I wish no service, good lady." He knelt beside
her. "I could not leave you in the well."

"You used your magic for my benefit, lord, and I
owe you magic in return. I can read your life-line
in the sticks. . . ." From the bosom of her ragged
dress she brought forth a bundle of polished wood-

en rods, each inscribed delicately with worn mystic symbols. She held them out to him in one hand, having dropped the meat to the grass before her; her other arm was hidden completely by her rags, as if guarding the place from which the sticks had been drawn.

"Then the villagers were right," said Mizella, recoiling a bit. "You *are* a witch."

A look of fear crossed the woman's face. "I have a skill, taught me by my mother, taught her by her mother before her. We are respected women in my homeland."

"You tell fortunes," said Alaric, and he reached out to reassure Mizella with a touch.

"Yes."

"Harbet said you were a midwife, that you killed his youngest child at birth."

She pulled the sticks back, close to her breast. "We are midwives in my family, and we read the life-line of every newborn babe. It was a sickly child—I needed no sticks to tell me it would die. I did not cause its death, but they put me in the well anyway. They blamed the bandits on me, and the recent drought, as if such things were under a poor old woman's control."

"I know they are not," said Alaric.

"I'm sure of that, lord, for you are a man of power. Shall I read your future?"

"No. I have no wish to know it, and I must find our supper now. Make ready to roast a chicken, Mizella."

"Don't forget to find a knife somewhere," she said. "I don't relish the notion of tearing its entrails out with my fingers."

He disappeared, and returned soon with a live chicken. "Courtesy of an old friend who mounts no guard on a well-locked coop." He produced a knife. "From a certain smithy."

The old woman stared at him with wide eyes and open mouth. "I thought we had flown," she whispered. "Lord, you are mighty indeed! Only once before have I seen magic such as this. The bane of my life! To think that it has saved me now. . . ."

"What do you mean?" said Alaric, his voice tense. This was the first person he had ever met who claimed to have seen his talent used before. He gripped her shoulder a bit too tightly. "You've seen someone go as I have done? Where? When?"

She gasped at the pain of his fingers. "Lord, my bones break easily!"

By a supreme act of will, he forced his fingers to relax. "Tell me," he said. "Oh, good lady, tell me!"

"It was years ago . . . a child . . . I delivered his mother of him, and as I slapped his rump to make him suck air and live, he screamed and . . . vanished."

"When? When?"

"His father was the Baron. He banished me forever from the land of my birth, and I have wandered ever since. Woe to the day I ever set foot in this land, where they fear my skill instead of respecting it!"

"When?" Alaric demanded. "When were you banished?"

She dropped the sticks into the grass before her knees and counted on them silently. "So long," she wailed. "Sixteen years have I wandered!"

"Sixteen years!" He glanced at Mizella, who had wrung the chicken's neck and now singed the feathers at the edge of the fire. She stopped for a moment.

"Why, Alaric," she murmured, *"you* are. . . ."

"Where is this country?" Alaric cried. "Do you know if the parents are still alive, if they have any other children? Tell me!'' He reached for her arms, to shake the information from her, and the sleeves of her garment fell back, revealing both arms completely for the first time. One was shorter than the other—it bore no hand.

The old woman jerked her arms away from him and hugged them to her bosom. ''He took my hand when he disappeared! He crippled me! He took my hand and caused the Baron to banish me! Oh, the blood, the blood! I thought I was going to die; the Baron made me thrust it into the fire to cauterize it, and then I wanted to die from the pain. . . .'' She bent over and rocked back and forth, weeping at the memory. ''I did nothing. Why did he banish me? He was not a superstitious man; he knew I was innocent. He must have known! He saw me cast no spell, make no magical motions. I was the victim and the child was the sorcerer!''

Hesitantly, Alaric moved closer to her, put his arms around her trembling shoulders. ''I . . . I'm sorry.'' His throat swelled shut, and he could barely choke out the words. ''It was I who did this to you. I was that child. I'm so sorry. . . .''

She lifted her head to stare uncomprehendingly.

''The slap—you say you slapped me—it must have startled and frightened me. I went without knowing how to use this power of mine. I was found naked on a hill far, far to the east of here, your hand still clutching my ankle. Your hand. . . .'' He held her tighter. ''Forgive me, forgive me, good lady. I didn't know . . . I couldn't know. . . .''

''You . . .'' she whispered. ''You . . . the child?''

''Yes. I'm sure of that.''

She gazed down at the stump of her arm. She touched it with her right hand, tucked the rags more closely about it. ''I owe you my life,'' she said. ''You

. . . the child?'' She peered into his face. ''Lord, you do resemble the Baron. What strange fortune it is . . . that you took my life away once, and now you give it back.''

Alaric nodded, unable to answer.

Mizella stood behind him, laid her hands on his head. ''Your mother, Alaric. You can find her now.''

''I can find her now,'' he echoed. ''Is she alive?''

''I don't know,'' said the old woman. ''I have been gone for sixteen years.''

''You'll take me home.''

''Oh, I can't! I was banished!''

''Think of it as a quest, a sixteen-year-long quest. And now you've found what you were searching for. Surely your exile will end when you bring it back.''

''I don't know.'' She raised her hand to her mouth, plucked at her lower lip.

He gripped that hand. ''Guide me home.''

''Home.'' She smiled suddenly. ''Yes, we'll go home. I'll see my sister, my brothers. . . .''

''Home,'' said Mizella, her fingers brushing Alaric's cheek. ''Home that you've never seen since the first moment of life. A baron's son. . . .''

''A baron's son,'' said Alaric. ''I wonder what kind of man the Baron is. And whether he'll want a witch for a child. . . .''

''He'll want a witch like you,'' Mizella said.

''I wonder.'' He leaned back against her and looked up into her face above his. ''I'm frightened,'' he said. ''But I'm going home anyway. Your intuition has been so accurate of late; what does it say about that?''

''It tells me you have great courage.''

''Or great stupidity.'' He smiled faintly. ''I hope I won't have to steal many more chickens along the way.''

But his mind, far from being concerned with chickens, was turning over the possibility that a baron's son might look to a king's daughter with a passion that was not completely hopeless.

The Lords
of All Power

WHILE YET A DAY'S MARCH AWAY, THE MINSTREL and his two companions sighted the castle. An imposing structure of crenelated walls and towers, it capped the highest hill in view and spread halfway down the slopes in three tiers of stone battlements. Impregnable was the first word that flashed through Alaric's mind. Except, of course, to such as he.

"There stands your father's capital," Artuva said, "just as it was seventeen years ago, just as it was before my father's father's time. Ten generations of Garlenon, they say, have held this land." A tinge of pride crept into her voice. "And my kin have served here for seasons beyond number." Then she recollected her long exile, a fact that sometimes escaped her aging mind, and she spoke more softly: "But I suppose those days are gone forever." She looked at the ground and muttered to herself, clutching the stump of her left hand close to her withered bosom.

Mizella stroked the old woman's thin hair, a soothing gesture she had often made in their months of travel. "You have brought back the Baron's son; surely he will reward you for that."

Artuva glanced up sideways, her mouth all pinched together. She considered Mizella's statement for a moment. "He is a hard man but fair. Perhaps there will be some reward. His grandsire rewarded me once with gold and jewels and a red house inside the Third Wall. But that was when I was young and beautiful like you, mistress, long before my crime.'' She shook her head. ''Just let me be with my folk—that is reward enough.''

Alaric squinted against the setting sun. He could barely discern the city, a sprawl of low buildings at the foot of the hill, half-hidden by intervening trees and rolling land. The smoke of many cooking fires hung above it, drifting slowly southward with the evening breeze.

''You'll see them tomorrow, if all goes well,'' he said. He looped Lightfoot's reins about a slender sapling, leaving enough slack that the horse might crop the fresh undergrowth. Though the season was full spring, Lightfoot's ribs still marked a winter of privation; his master had not dared steal enough grain to keep him well-fed. Yet he had carried two riders at once, through long days and miles with little sign of fatigue; he was bred a war-horse, bred to bear an armored man and his weapons, and two unencumbered bodies were a small load for him. He lowered his head and fed, ignoring the bustle of camp-making that eddied around him.

Old Artuva set about gathering wood as Alaric vanished in search of provisions. She had quickly become accustomed to the young minstrel's private mode of travel, accepting its reality with a careful respect but no outward sign of fear. Unlike Mizella, she dismissed all belief in the Dark One, insisting that magical powers were merely another skill, like singing or weaving, that some people acquired easily and others could never master. In her country, she said, magic was a commonplace of life; fortune-telling, spells, philters, the manufacture of luck charms—nearly everyone had a secret or two that he revealed only to his dearest children. Even the Baron, his subjects agreed, must practice some art that enabled him to vanquish his enemies, though whether spell, philter, foreknowledge, or charm, no one knew.

"Tribute comes to him from far beyond the horizon," she murmured, staring into the fire that Mizella tended—staring into the past. "Finely wrought ornaments of red gold and gems, gossamer cloth bordered in purple, richly carven furnishings of dark wood, well-matched teams of handsome horses. I saw a caravan once of strange spindly-legged animals, piled high with bags and baskets, driven by leather-skinned men who beat them with flails. The Baron himself came out to meet them at the gate of the Third Wall. And I thought to myself, he rules the whole world—towns beyond number, the people and their animals, the crops they raise and the ores they mine, the very air they breathe." The popping of a green twig brought her back to the present, and she looked up; Alaric had returned with a large round cheese and a fresh-baked loaf of bread which Mizella sliced for dinner.

"Where I come from," said Mizella, "we never heard of him." She passed the old woman a share of the food.

Artuva nodded. "I was only a child then. Later, I learned from elders, from travelers, how vast was the world and how small a corner of it my liege lord controlled. And yet . . . I had to walk far indeed to obey his banishment. I no longer recall how many towns I passed that bore his black and scarlet emblem." She nibbled at her cheese, looking back over her shoulder at the castle, now a looming shadow on the darkening sky. "He has surely added more since then, for his

House was ever victorious in battle. And ever desirous of new land.''

Mizella made a sign to ward off evil. "Perhaps headman Harbet was not mistaken to decorate his village with guardian symbols.''

"They will not help him if Garlenon wants it. His House is proof against magic. My father's cousin told a tale of the great sorcerer employed by one of the Baron's enemies, of the spells and charms he tried, of a waxen image he molded and slashed with silver blades. The sorcerer was slain, and his lord, too, but Garlenon suffered not at all.''

Alaric glanced at Mizella, eyebrows raised. He had told her often, though never convinced her entirely, that ceremonial magic was a fraud. This story seemed new evidence for his view. "Harbet is probably safe enough because of sheer distance, not to mention the dearth of value in his village. A man bent on conquest could find far worthier prizes. The Baron must have a sizable army, eh?''

Artuva shrugged. "I do not know.''

"What then? Does he march to war in dead of night when no one may see?''

The old woman shook her head. "I have seen him ride off with a small retinue and return triumphant. But I have never seen a large army.''

"It must be garrisoned elsewhere. Surely he's taken your sons and brothers to fight his battles. Or hires mercenaries.''

"Our men have never gone to war for him. He fights with magic; some say he conjures soldiers out of the earth—soldiers that disappear with the dawn. But I've never seen that. When my mother's mother was a child, the city was besieged by a force of ten thousand men. The Baron gathered the people within the Third Wall for three days; on the fourth, the enemy dispersed of their own accord, and the people went back to their homes. Many rumors arose after that: of swords that wielded themselves, of men driven to suicide by terrifying apparitions—but these were only speculation. From dusk to dawn for those three nights, a light burned in the high tower, the Baron's own apartments. What he did there, no man of the city knew, but it was enough. The House of Garlenon needs no army."

Alaric could imagine what had happened—the power of instantaneous travel was the well-guarded art of the Garlenons. He wondered how many of his relatives possessed it.

"What is he like?" Alaric said. "My father."

"Who? Oh, yes." Her eyes focused on him. "The Baron, your father. He is tall and dark, like you, though heavier in the body, and he wore a full black beard when last I saw him. He was some thirty years old then and had been Baron for five or six of them. He was a fair man, a just man. He always treated me well, even at the last. He could have put me to death, but he's not like that, not like his grandsire. The *old* Baron had a man publicly flogged who refused him a daughter. The man was crippled, the daughter never seen again. Some said she ran off with a suitor, but a laundress I knew once claimed to see a red chemise embroidered with her name hanging in the courtyard— so it seemed she must serve the Baron's pleasure after all. Years passed, other women came and went, but *she*. . . . Yes, we wondered if he had killed her, though no one dared speak such words aloud. Her poor bones lying far from her family—all for the foolishness of a father."

Mizella moved closer to Alaric, slipped her shoulders under his cloak. "The present Baron is different, you say."

"Oh, yes; quite different. At least, toward his own subjects. Toward his enemies, he is as ruthless as his ancestors were."

"We are not his enemies," said Alaric.

He leaned back against the thick bole of an ancient oak, one arm cuddling Mizella's warmth to his side. His free hand plucked randomly at the strings of his new lute; after losing the old one to the cleansing fire of self-righteous witch-haters, he had searched diligently for another as like it as possible. In a marketplace somewhere west of Durman's realm, he found an instrument of similar style . . . battered and worn, missing pegs and strings and much of its varnish, the neck half cracked off. Pretending an idle interest, he convinced the merchant who owned it—no musician himself—that it was worthless except as a possible wall decoration. The merchant alleged that he discovered it under a fall of timbers in the ruins of a wealthy house, the last portable item of any value there, somehow overlooked by bandits and scavengers alike; it had cost him nothing and he was willing to sell it for pittance. Alaric had no money but traded his spare shirt for the instrument. That night he carved fresh pegs from Lightfoot's stirrups, the only seasoned wood available. A few days later, at a more westerly market, he bartered the rest of the saddle for solvent, varnish, and glue, as well as costly new strings.

"You needn't sell the saddle," Mizella had chided. "I can soon earn enough by . . . by plying my old trade."

"And I can cast the fortune-sticks for passersby in the square," offered Artuva.

Alaric shook his head. "The lute is mine, the saddle is mine. I will not require you to rent out your body, Mizella, nor you to chance again the cry of witchcraft, good lady. If things go well, we can buy a new saddle someday. Till then, Lightfoot will move all the faster for being less encumbered.''

"You could have sold the sword," Mizella whispered. She refrained from suggesting that he steal either money or materials, well aware of his distaste for theft beyond bare necessity. "The scabbard alone would fetch a greater price than the saddle."

"No, I'll not sell the sword."

The sword was the single memento left to him of a passage in his life that he wished never to forget, yet remembered too well. Solinde. . . . He hoped she sometimes looked westward from her tower to meditate on the fate of her minstrel. Her embroidered favor had perished in the flames with his lute— her favor, far more precious to him than the lute itself, though the lute was a relic of his days with Dall. Now he had nothing of his beloved but a memory.

A baron's son, though, might dream of more. . . . He smiled and thought of Solinde even as he held Mizella in his arms.

An early start brought them to the city walls by mid-afternoon. The city itself had spread far beyond the old stone ramparts; undefended shops and homes and streets of hard-packed earth demonstrated the security that Garlenon's people enjoyed. The shops were crowded with elegant goods, domestic and foreign— cloth of every color and degree of opacity; wines in gaily painted flagons and tinted glass decanters; intricate ornaments and prismatic gems; household utensils of polished metal and finely carved wood; fresh, common foodstuffs and exotic preserves wholly unknown to Alaric. Shops and homes alike were not merely sturdy and serviceable but large and opulent, many boasting two and three doors, half a dozen windows, slatted shutters and sculpted lintels, walls of varicolored inlaid tile, and patios of neatly dressed stone. The people who hurried on their errands or lazed in open-air wineshops were attired like brilliant birds, bedecked with buttons, studs, and flashing trinkets, broad leather belts and square-toed, high-heeled, silver-buckled shoes. Even the horses sported trappings of every hue, plumes and tassels twined in mane and tail. Alaric felt shabby as he passed among them, lacking even a clean shirt.

The three travelers walked, Mizella leading Lightfoot. "This city has never been sacked," she muttered. Her eyes were caught by the feminine finery on every side, and she brushed at her hair and tried to smooth the wrinkles in her dirty gown.

"Not since my mother's mother's time," said Artuva. "Lord Garlenon protects us well and rarely keeps all the tribute for himself. Come—the house of my kin lies just beyond the wall."

"After seventeen years," Mizella whispered aside to the minstrel, "I hope they are still there."

"Only she was banished," he replied softly. "And the Baron, she keeps saying, is a fair man. Would a fair man have punished an entire family for the crime of a single member?"

"Sometimes I wonder if she knows which Baron she speaks of—the present one, his father, or his grandfather. Her mind. . . ."

"If a newborn babe had vanished with your hand, perhaps your mind would also wander on occasion."

Artuva led them through the wide, iron-banded gate. Beyond the wall, the city was older, the buildings more closely packed but no less elaborately decorated. Traffic was denser here on the main thoroughfare, and the newcomers had to march single file, holding hands, dodging horses and oxcarts and wandering sweetmeat vendors whose sharp-cornered trays were almost as lethal as knives. Fortunately, the old woman soon turned into a narrow side street and then into a second, and the crush of people lessened considerably.

"This is the Street of Four Blacksmiths," said Artuva. She gestured toward the second house from the corner, a two-story stone and wood structure, its wide main door inlaid with burnished copper disks. "I was born here, and here I live with my eldest brother's family and my unmarried sister. See, there is our mark over the door."

A pair of cats chasing a duck—all most lifelike— were rendered in bas-relief on the lintel.

As Alaric tied Lightfoot to the hitching ring set in the wall, Artuva began to search among her rags, in pockets, sleeves, and folds of cloth. She fumbled for some time, whimpering, "My key . . . my key . . . I seem to have lost my key. Besk will be furious. He'll have to change the lock."

Alaric took her arm. "I don't think you need worry about that. Shall we knock?"

"Oh, yes. Someone is usually home."

Stepping up to the door, Alaric knocked. While he waited for an answer, he noted that the copper disks in the panel bore figures and scenes delicately engraved. If he had not seen an abundance of similar ornamentation in the rest of the city, he would think that Artuva came of a wealthy house. He had never visited such a city, not elsewhere in Garlenon's realm, not in Durman, not even in Royale, which was judged rich by eastern standards. This, he told himself, was truly a conqueror's capital.

The door opened, and a tall, balding middle-aged man looked out. "Yes?" he said.

Artuva squinted at him. "Who are you?"

"I am the head of this household, Orpether by name," he said.

"Head? Where is Besk? Where is my brother Besk?"

Orpether stared at her for a long moment. "My father Besk is in his grave."

"Grave?" Her mouth opened wide, and she wailed. "Oh, Besk, my Besk!" One-handed, she tore at her thin white hair until Mizella made her stop. "Seventeen years!" she moaned. "Seventeen years! Oh, my Besk!" She raised her arms in supplication. "And my sister Vinta . . . she, too. . . ?"

Orpether glanced up and down the street, then reached out and gently took Artuva by the shoulder. "I think you'd best come inside." He looked from Alaric to Mizella, gestured for them to follow as well.

Beyond the door was a chamber furnished with sumptuous upholstered chairs and small tables of patterned wood; Orpether bade them all sit, and he himself took the chair nearest the old woman's. She did not weep, but sat with downcast eyes and slumping shoulders.

"You are . . . Artuva?" Orpether said, his tone incredulous.

She nodded. Her face was pinched and tired, and the corners of her mouth sagged.

He touched her hand. "I am your nephew. I had just married when you were . . . when you left."

"I remember the wedding," she muttered. "Besk was there. He danced till dawn."

"He died two years ago, Aunt Artuva. But Aunt

Vinta is still with us, in vigorous health. She's out at market now and should return soon."

Artuva sighed. "He was such a handsome man, my dear brother."

"My eldest daughter shall draw a bath for you, Aunt, and lay out fresh clothes. Are you hungry? We have soup on the fire this very moment. I'll see to it." He hurried out of the room.

"He was the best of us all," Artuva murmured.

Mizella knelt beside the old woman's chair. "Your sister is well, and your nephew and his family. Dear lady, you knew that some things would be changed after so many years."

Artuva glanced at her, then at Alaric. "Seventeen years. Yes, some things have changed indeed. Besk has died, I have gotten old, and you, lord, have grown from a babe to a man. Shall we go to your father now?"

Alaric smiled. "We are hardly dressed for presentation at court. I have waited so many years; another day will matter little."

She plucked at her rags. "Forgive me, lord; I had forgotten I was so ill-clothed. That is an old woman's curse—forgetfulness. But *this* I cannot forget." She touched the stump of her left hand. "We go to the castle in the morning."

"Good lady, I think it would be better if I went alone, a poor minstrel to entertain my lord Baron. You and Mizella should stay here while I see what a minstrel's eyes can see."

"What, wary of your own father? Did I not say he was a fair man? You'll find he is not like his grandsire."

"I hope for the best."

Artuva's nephew and his thirteen-year-old daughter came in with bowls of thick, steaming soup and chunks of dark bread still warm from the oven. "You must tell us of your travels, Aunt—where you went and what manner of people you encountered," Orpether said. "You look well. Father feared you would wander the world hungry and cold; he sent a packet of clothes and money with one of the neighbor boys, but the lad rode three days and found no trace of you."

Artuva dipped up the soup with a silver spoon. "They took me far and fast. For a time I did wander the world hungry and cold, but lately Alaric and Mizella have been caring for me, and I have eaten well and slept warm."

Orpether inclined his head in Alaric's direction. "For my aunt's sake, sir, my house is yours."

Shortly after the food had been consumed, Vinta returned from her shopping, and there was a tearful reunion between the old women, followed by a bath and a change of clothing for Artuva. Mizella and Alaric toured the house with one of Orpether's sons, a lad of twelve, and they answered his eager questions about the world beyond Garlenon. Inevitably, the minstrel was asked for a song.

"I should sing for the lady of the house," he told the boy, "in thanks for her hospitality."

"Aunt Vinta won't care. She's nearly deaf."

"I mean your mother."

"Oh, she died when my little sister was born."

"Ah," said Alaric, and so he sang of the orphan prince who ruled a vast empire at an early age when all he really wanted was to wander the woods in search of butterflies. Four other children—three younger, one older than his guide—heard the music and came to form a ring about the singer. They listened, wide-eyed, to tales of goblins, elves, and unicorns until their father announced bedtime.

"You must tell them," Orpether said aside to Alaric, "that such creatures are imaginary. There is enough magic in the world without them."

Alaric shrugged. "There is magic in song, but precious little in the world. Surely your children understand the difference between the one and the other."

Orpether frowned at him. "In this part of the world, there is magic aplenty. I have heard that it is not so in other places."

"It is not so in most places."

"Well, we have advantages here that the rest of the world, it seems, does not."

"That is certainly true," Alaric said, gazing around the room at the colorful hangings and padded furniture. "I have been in castles that boasted fewer advantages."

"I suppose, then, that you have no special skill." The emphasis he placed on the last word made his meaning clear.

Alaric suppressed a smile. "None that I would call magic."

"You visit the castle tomorrow?"

"Yes."

"My eldest daughter can read the sticks for you."

"No. The lady Artuva offered that many a time, but I don't care to foresee the future. It will come as it comes, and I'll deal with it on that basis."

"One of our neighbors makes charms—they are quite inexpensive. . . ."

"No. I depend on my lute and my voice, thank you."

"The Baron is a man of great power."

"So I have been told. Men of great power tend to be rich; minstrels tend to be poor. Perhaps we can achieve some sort of equilibrium."

Orpether shook his head. "We do not bother the Baron. He has his own affairs, and we have ours. He keeps us safe, and we perform occasional services for him; he asks little."

"You are afraid of him."

"I would not visit him lightly. Especially without protection."

"My lack of gold is not a light matter to me." He laid a hand on Orpether's shoulder. "I am moved by your concern, my good host, but I think you worry unnecessarily."

"Dig your own grave, minstrel. I warn you only for my aunt's sake." Shaking his head, he turned and walked away.

Alaric and Mizella slept that night wrapped in a fluffy feather comforter on the sitting-room floor.

"I'll come back, or else I'll send for you when I know how the wind blows," he said, after the rest of the household had retired.

She stroked his face. "Poor minstrel. You don't know what to do with me, do you? I am hardly a fit companion for a baron's son."

"There's none here that knows your past."

"*We* know, Alaric, and that is enough." She leaned over him, a dark shape in the dark room. "I release you from any obligation to me. You have earned my bread long enough; there is no need for you to do more than you have already done."

"Mizella—"

She stopped his words with her fingers. "My dearest minstrel, we are not tied together in any way. Go up to the castle; don't worry about me."

He gripped her hand. "Mizella, in a strange land—"

"But not among strangers, I think. Artuva's family is kind. Orpether has been without a wife for several years; if there were a woman he knew that was free and pleased him, he would have remarried before now. I am not unaware of my own attractions, Alaric. If you go up to the castle and become the Baron's son . . . Orpether will know soon enough that I am no longer yours.'' She kissed his cheek. ''Dear Alaric, anyone with eyes in his head knows that we are a mismated pair. Who could blame us for finding other, more appropriate partners?''

''You hardly know the man!''

''If not him, then another. It is a large city and rich; I think I could spend an easy lifetime here.'' She paused for a long moment, her lips close to his face. ''We have been partners in despair; now, I see better times coming for both of us. We must be practical, dear minstrel. I know you still dream of her. Well, I have dreams, too. You have been good to me, and I have tried to be good to you, but we both know it was never love.''

He was silent, felt her breath against his hair, her fingers light on his neck. ''No,'' he said at last. ''It was never love.''

''Then hold me close, and we will bid farewell in the best possible manner.''

In the morning, their host served a hearty breakfast. ''Allow me to loan you a fresh shirt,'' he said to Alaric.

The minstrel shrugged. ''It would look quite out of place with my other garments.'' He dusted his worn and faded cloak with a borrowed brush, and then he shined his boots. ''I'm a poor traveling minstrel, and I don't mind looking the part. I could use a fresh feather for my cap, though. This one has hardly a vane left.'' One of the children ran to fetch a green neck feather from a neighbor's goose. ''My face is clean, my hands washed, and my lute polished

to a high luster. What more does a minstrel need?
I thank you for your hospitality, and for your advice, good Orpether. And thank you, lady Artuva,"
and he bent and kissed her gnarled hand, "for everything. . . ."

Artuva wore a clean gown today, and a silken ban-
deau in her hair—she was quite transformed from the
pitiful wanderer of other days, and she even seemed
to stand straighter. "Fare you well, young master,"
she said. "I've read the sticks for you, and I know you
will fare well."

He smiled at the old woman's faith in nonsense.
Then he turned to Mizella and kissed her cheek. "Take
care of this one, my host."

Mizella smiled, both at Alaric and Orpether.

Orpether said, "I hope to see you again, young
man."

Out on the street, though the hour was early, the
crowd was already thick, flowing in a single direction—to the nearest marketplace. Alaric mounted
Lightfoot and pressed toward the hill, against the traffic. A few other men rode horseback here and there,
but most of the citizens walked, their smaller bodies
slipping through openings in the throng that no horse
could negotiate. Eventually, Alaric and Lightfoot
moved into less populous areas.

Nearer the castle walls—indeed, on the very slope
of the hill itself, the city ended abruptly, yielding to a
no-man's-land of hard-packed barren earth and, just
below the first tier of battlements, a dry moat partially
obliterated by an accumulation of dirt and debris. Instead of a drawbridge there was a short causeway of
dressed stone, and at the far end of the causeway, a
portcullis barred the entrance to the castle. Just visible
beyond the gate, two armored but helmetless men
sat at a small table, playing at dice. They noticed

Alaric before he reached the portcullis, and they stood up, halberds in hand, and stared at him as he approached.

They might have been brothers, so strong was the facial and bodily resemblance between them. Their highly polished armor showed the Baron's crest on back and breastplate: two red chevrons on a black shield. The same emblem was bolted to naked stone above the entrance.

"Good day," said Alaric, and he dismounted to bow and doff his cap.

"Good day," said one of the men.

"Allow me to introduce myself: I am Alaric, purveyor of songs and master of the lute. I seek audience with the lord of this castle that I may brighten his dinner table and fill his evenings with days of yore, with knights and dragons and maidens fair. From beyond the eastern forest I have come to offer my skills, which, I say in all modesty, are not inconsiderable. May I plead my case before him, gentles?"

The men looked at each other, their expressions bland. "You sing," said the one who had acknowledged the greeting.

"Exactly. I sing most excellently well, sir. Kings have given me gold and lesser men their daughters in return for my songs."

They eyed his travel-worn state and raised their eyebrows skeptically. "Then why have you left those places to come here?"

"Wanderlust," Alaric said, smiling broadly. "New cities, new faces. The world is wide."

"Well, then, you'd better get on if you want to see the rest of it before you die." The two turned away from the portcullis and sat down to their game once more.

"But wait!" cried Alaric. "Your lord will surely enjoy my skills . . . and I would greatly appreciate a little food and comfort on my journey."

"There's food and comfort aplenty in the city."

"Ah, but not like that of the castle."

The guard who had not yet spoken looked up lazily. "We have no need of minstrels here."

Alaric's fingers curled around the thick iron bars. "Have you the authority to keep me out? Is there no one to whom I may appeal? I come highly recommended. I'll give you a sample of my wares. . . ." He unslung the lute and strummed a tentative chord, but he had not yet opened his mouth to sing when a halberd clanged sharply against the portcullis.

"Leave off, boy," said the first guard. "No one enters the castle without special permission of the Baron, and I am sure he won't be interested in a minstrel. Especially not a minstrel."

His partner nodded. "Sing in the markets," he advised. "You'll find plenty of silver there."

"Gentles," said Alaric, "I had hoped to sing before the greatest lords of the earth, insofar as I could find them. The Baron, I have heard, is greater than all the others I have entertained. How could I hold my head up among my fellow minstrels if I passed through his territory without singing for him?"

"We have our orders, boy. Go away or you'll wish you had."

Alaric did not have to feign dejection as he turned Lightfoot about and led him back toward the city. He hadn't expected to be turned away—minstrels rarely were. To reassure himself, he found a nearby inn, where the proprietor was glad enough to trade a cup of wine for a song. Alaric took the drink out onto the flagstone patio, where four heavy wooden tables testified to the continuing good weather. He sat in a hard-backed chair, leaned his elbows on a table, and stared up at the castle, which dominated the view from his vantage. Rising high above the concentric walls was the keep, a tall tower with crenelated parapet and many window slits. Alaric's practiced eye measured the distance to one of those windows; the perch was a precarious one, and even if he essayed it—what then? He tried to think of some other way to enter the castle innocently.

Presently, as he was nursing his cup and gazing out into the street at the passing traffic, he heard young voices raised in simple, two-part harmony. He glanced this way and that and saw them finally: six small dark-haired children—the eldest no more than seven or eight—walking down the main street, holding hands and singing. Every one of them was clothed all in black but for two red chevrons sewn on the breast and back of his short-sleeved tunic. They skipped up to the portcullis and were admitted immediately. Soon, their song faded in the distance.

A customer of the inn, a grizzled old man who had been sitting at a table at the far end of the patio since Alaric's arrival, moved to a nearer chair. He sported pearls in both ears and a cravat of multicolored silk tucked into a soft blue tunic. Anywhere in the more familiar world, Alaric would have judged him rich, but here he was certainly just an average citizen. He smiled.

"I'll buy your second cup of wine," he said. "It was a fine song."

"Thank you, sir," replied Alaric, and he motioned to the landlord to comply with the old man's offer.

"Stranger, are you not?"

Alaric nodded.

"Your clothes give you away."

The minstrel glanced from his patron's wealthy attire to his own worn gear. "They are the only clothes I have, sir."

The old man held up a hand. "I meant no offense, young stranger."

"Then no offense is taken." Alaric lifted his freshened cup in a silent toast, which the old man answered in kind, and together they quaffed red wine in the morning sun.

"I sit here often," the old man said. "I watch the chevroned children come out of that gate to play, and I watch the carts of tribute go in to be counted by our lord Baron. Today . . . I saw you turned away."

"Indeed, I was turned away. I offered song and was rejected." He laughed dryly. "I am not accustomed to that. My songs have always been good enough for all manner of high-born folk, for kings and princes."

The old man rubbed his clean-shaven chin with thumb and forefinger.

"Well, it is not an easy task to enter that gate. One must have business within."

"I had business. Or, at least, I offered entertainment. Surely that is business enough."

"Ah, perhaps if you had a dancing bear or could stand on your head and walk on your hands, you would have business in the castle, but song . . . young stranger, you heard those children, did you not?"

"I heard them."

"And so does the rest of the city, regularly, every time they come out to the street. I think perhaps those in the castle have enough of song."

Alaric fingered his lute. "I doubt those children know the sort of songs I would offer."

The old man shrugged.

"When the guard changes," said Alaric, "I will try again."

The old man's eyebrows rose. "I would not be so eager to pass through that portal."

"Is there something to fear within?"

He lowered his voice. "I have no certain knowledge, you must understand . . . but some say the Baron has a glass of rare workmanship that enables him to see the four corners of the earth, to hear men's very thoughts, to strike an enemy dead by speaking his name. Myself, I take care to harbor no thoughts which would excite his interest."

Alaric played a simple melody on the lute, but he sang no words, only hummed in counterpoint. "Good sir," he said at last, "I have never visited a city where the people feared their lord so greatly. Yet you are all rich and busy, and you smile at each other as you pass on the street."

The old man sipped the last of his wine as he considered his answer. "It is a habit of mind, I think. Our fathers feared his father, our grandfathers feared his grandfather, and so we fear him. Can one feel otherwise toward a man whose hands hold the power of life and death?"

"One can. Other citizens in other cities love their lords."

"Ah, love. Yes, we do love him, for he gives us peace and justice. But fear is by far a stronger emotion."

"And when he comes out into the city—do you cheer him or hide your faces?"

"He rarely comes out."

"And when he does?"

"We stand respectful, of course. He has never asked for other behavior."

Alaric stared up at the castle. "He must be a lonely man."

"I doubt it. He has plenty of company up there."

''I was told that his family has ruled this land for ten generations.''

The old man closed his eyes and seemed to count silently. ''That sounds like an accurate figure.''

''It must have been a wild territory at one time, to require such a castle.''

''Yes, lad . . . long, long ago. The castle is much older than my lord Baron's family. It was here before the city, before the earliest citizen built his mud hut at the base of the hill. See that squat, crumbling building below the Third Wall—the outermost wall?'' He pointed with a bony finger to a jagged-topped structure that was streaked dark with the soot and dust of many years, darker by far than the castle itself. ''There is the original keep, or so it is said, built no one knows how long ago, built into the very side of the hill.''

Alaric squinted at the indicated building. ''I have never seen a keep built on the *side* of a hill.''

''You're thinking it a poor fortification, that it ought to be at the top.''

''Exactly.''

''Well,'' and the old man leaned back in his chair and gazed meditatively at the hillside, ''they say that the slope was steeper in those days, and not so grassy. They say the crest was unassailable. And, of course, the far side is almost sheer. No, that was as high as the old builders could reach, it seems. Not really a bad fortification; it commands the valley, yields a good view of the foothills. One can probably see as far as the river at that height. They call it the Castle Under the Hill.''

''To distinguish it from the castle on top of the hill.''

''Yes.''

''It looks in poor repair.''

''It is a ruin, uninhabited for generations. The Baron's ancestors abandoned it when they completed their own keep at the crest—what a task *that* must have been!''

''He should tear it down.''

''Ah, no. There is a legend about it, that the castle on top of the hill will never be taken as long as the Castle Under the Hill stands. So you see, he leaves it. A careful man, our lord.''

Alaric shook his head. ''A legend.''

The old man looked at Alaric sidewise. ''Who knows what truth there is in legends? My grandfather once suggested that the source of the Garlenon power was in that ruined keep. It is well-sealed with brick and steel to prevent the curious from investigating.''

''Were I the Baron, I would remove the source of my power to safer storage within the walls of my castle.''

The old man smiled. ''We have many legends, many rumors in this city. Perhaps you'll set some of them to music during your stay. The guard changes after the noonday meal. If you pass your cap among the bachelors who will gather here to eat, you may find your songs earning enough to compensate you somewhat for being turned away again.''

''You think I'll be turned away again?''

''You think not? The guards are the lord Baron's cousins. They know his mind.''

''His cousins?''

''Yes. Every one of them.''

Alaric sighed. ''I suppose I must practice walking on my hands then.''

The old man laughed.

After the meal, during which Alaric did indeed acquire a substantial number of coins, the old man bade him farewell and went off on some business of his

own. The inn, which had been virtually empty all
morning, filled when the landlord began to bring out
plates of steaming stew and buttered noodles, and it
stayed full for the afternoon as men came and went,
ate and drank and diced at the tables. Alaric sang and
sang again, and his cap waxed heavy with money, not
just copper and silver, but gold as well. He sang of
love and death and high adventure in exotic lands
where the trees bore purple leaves, the grass grew red
as blood, and the men were four-armed giants. He
sang of winged horses and speaking fish and rivers of
wine. He sang for drunks and sober men, for women
and their young children, and for a pair of youths who
insisted they, too, could play the lute; but he refused
to surrender the instrument to their fancies and never
knew if their claims were true.

Toward evening, he tired, and even the offer of a
cup of wine could not persuade him to continue. His
voice was still clear and light, but he knew his limi-
tations, and he could judge by the state of his throat
that they were fast approaching.

"Tomorrow is another day," he said, and he went
out on the patio to sit in the fading sunlight. He gazed
up at the castle and wondered if he should try for ad-
mission again or wait till the morrow. He was still
sitting thus and musing when the young woman arrived.

She was tall and slender, dark-haired and dark-eyed,
though pale-skinned; she might have been a sister
to the guards at the gate. She wore a full-skirted, long-
sleeved black dress ornamented only by the double red
chevrons splashed across its close-fitting bodice.

"You are the minstrel who sought entrance to the
castle this morning?" she asked.

Alaric stood up, bowed deeply. "I am."

She stared long at his face, her eyes narrowed. "What is your name?"

"Alaric."

"Where are you from?"

"Everywhere. But principally, the east, beyond the great forest."

"I am the lady Dejarnemir. You are to come with me."

"To where, my lady?"

She nodded toward the castle. "You wished to enter, did you not?"

"Yes, my lady." He picked up his lute and followed her into the street. Draping Lightfoot's reins over his shoulder, he let the horse amble behind them.

The woman walked swiftly and surely, without looking back, and the portcullis rose smoothly at her approach. The new guardsmen greeted her and stood aside to let her pass; they strongly resembled the earlier pair, and Alaric could well believe that guards and woman alike came of a single family. He wondered if he resembled them; he had never seen his face in a good mirror and had only Artuva's word that he favored the Baron. Had Dejarnemir stared so long because it was true?

Within the Third Wall was a shady courtyard invisible from the city; a grassy lawn and low trees flanked the flagstone stairway that led uphill to the massive Second Wall. Beyond the greenery, the space between ramparts was crowded with two-story structures of pale stone and red-painted wood, their windows festooned with flowers, their walls with ivy, the peaks of their shingled red roofs rearing almost into the dimming sunlight.

Brightly painted benches and tables were scattered among the trees, and groups of merrymakers clustered about them, talking, laughing, and drinking from

crystal and silver goblets. Some of these folk wore
black and red garments like Dejarnemir's, but most
were dressed in colorful finery garnished with gems
and gold. Of the latter, three only did not bear the
stamp of the Baron's household on their faces—three
women no less richly garbed than their fellows, one
fair-haired, one swarthy-skinned, the third a blazing
redhead. They sat together, a trio of beauties, and
though their costumes differed in every detail of style,
color, and trim, each of them wore upon her breast
the selfsame thick gold chain and heart-shaped ruby
pendant. They alone of the throng inclined their heads
as Dejarnemir passed; the others waved or smiled or
merely watched.

A small boy came down the stairway to take charge
of Lightfoot, and he led the horse away along a flagstone path that wound between the red-roofed buildings.

Alaric and his guide climbed to the top of the steps.

"Earlier, I was turned away, my lady," he said.
"Why am I invited in now, and who am I bound to
see?"

Her gaze skimmed over his body, lit on his face and
held there. "The men you spoke to mistook the Baron's pleasure. If you do indeed come from beyond the
eastern forest, you may be able to offer us a few new
songs."

"A hundred. The farther I wander, the fewer of my
songs are known to my listeners."

She shrugged, a tiny, almost indetectable movement of head and shoulders. "We know a good many
here."

"I heard the children singing a simple rhyme. There
are other songs, more complex, more interesting—"

"Children must begin with simple music. Come."
She turned to the iron-banded gate of the Second Wall,

which was shut tight. At her sharp knock, the guard within slowly swung it open.

Their route was totally enclosed now, a long flight of steps leading ever upward, broken by the broad level spaces of cross-corridors. Oil lamps on either wall illuminated the high-ceilinged stone staircase, casting weird, multiple shadows on the walls and floors. A few people moved here, and all of these bore the familial resemblance that Alaric had noted on so many faces. One or two greeted Dejarnemir with a nod, but none stopped to speak.

A dozen steps below the summit, she paused, breathing heavily. "The main hall is before us, and you will meet the Baron there. I suggest that you kneel."

A short curved corridor opened into a large room crowded with rows of long tables and straight-backed chairs and hung with tapestries and gleaming weapons. High narrow windows admitted the remnants of late afternoon light, which was augmented by oil lamps mounted at wide intervals along the walls. On a dais opposite the doorway rested an ornately carved table of ebony, thickly gilded; two people sat there in chairs that might better be termed thrones: the man was near fifty, powerfully built and tall, his dark hair and beard shot with gray; the woman might have been a few years younger, was equally tall, a more mature version of Dejarnemir. She could have been the Baron's sister, but Alaric guessed that she was his cousin and his wife. When she caught sight of the minstrel, she sat a little straighter in her chair—a subdued reaction, but one that told Alaric everything: this was his mother, and she knew him.

He approached the dais and knelt.

"Here is the minstrel, lord," said Dejarnemir.

Baron Garlenon rose slowly and walked around the table for a closer view. "Stand up, boy."

Alaric stood.

"What is your name?" His eyes drank in the minstrel's face.

"Alaric, lord."

"How old are you?"

"Seventeen, come this summer."

"Where were you born?"

"I was a foundling, lord, and grew up in the village of Garthem in the land of Amberstow, far to the east of the great eastern forest."

The Baron looked over his shoulder at the woman. "What say you, cousin?"

She joined him, standing so close to Alaric that her long skirt brushed his boots. "I say the test."

The Baron plucked at his beard. "It may be pure coincidence."

"It is not."

"Lorenta, I would rather let him go his way than see him fail the test."

"He will not fail." She touched Alaric's hair gently, felt of its texture with thumb and forefinger. "He will not fail."

"You are too sure."

"He is a minstrel."

The Baron sighed. "Yes, he is a minstrel."

Lorenta put her hand beneath Alaric's chin and turned his face to profile. "Young singer, are you our child?" Her tone was peremptory, compelling, and Alaric found himself discarding the last shreds of an inclination to masquerade.

"Yes, my lady, I am."

"How do you know?"

"Artuva, the midwife who attended my birth, told me."

The Baron shook his head. "A chance resemblance, and she told him he could wring gold from it."

"I was found on a hillside, newborn and naked, and a bloody, severed hand was clutching my ankles. My foster parents always assumed that magic was involved somehow. When Artuva told me her story and showed me the stump of her hand, I knew who I was. She said I resembled you, and I am the proper age. Who else can I be?"

"Who else indeed," said the Baron, "except an imposter?"

"The test, cousin," said his consort.

"You claim to be our child. Very well. There is a test which will prove or disprove that claim. Will you attempt it, or will you leave my domain this day and never return?"

"I will attempt any test you set me, lord."

"Then come with me." A stone stairway curved upward along one wall of the great room; the Baron began to climb, and Alaric, Lorenta, and Dejarnemir—with a candle—followed closely.

Their destination was a narrow, windowless, hearthless cubicle. The wavering flame of the candle revealed unadorned gray walls and a bare floor; just beyond the threshold, a circle was inscribed in black on the smooth stone underfoot. While the ladies hung back, the Baron walked to the far end of the room and motioned Alaric to join him. The young minstrel had hardly obeyed when close-set iron bars descended from the ceiling to separate him from the door.

"There is only one way out of this room, my supposed child," said the Baron. "Do not bother to search for loose stones hiding secret passages or windows or some trapdoor beneath the bars—there are none of those things here. One way only, and if you cannot discover it, you must stay in this room till you die.''

Alaric looked at the Baron. ''You are sealed in as well.''

''I was,'' said the Baron, and he vanished. A draft brushed Alaric—air rushing to fill the void where a body had been.

''Come to me, Alaric,'' the Baron said from beyond the bars. He pointed to the black circle at his feet. ''If you be a true Garlenon, come here.''

Alaric smiled, and he was there.

The Baron laid his hand on Alaric's shoulder. ''Welcome home.''

Alaric felt his throat tighten, and he spoke haltingly. ''I was afraid . . . that I was a freak.''

His mother stepped close, linked her arm in his. ''We are all freaks, Alaric. Every soul of Garlenon— your cousins all—can do that which you have just done.''

''True,'' said the Baron, ''but none of us could do it at birth. We found our power later, the boys when they sprouted beards, the girls when they first came under the Moon's influence. We thought, when you vanished at birth, that we had lost you forever, for how could a newborn babe envision some destination other than . . . nothingness? But you lived, and you have returned to us. It was well, then, that I banished Artuva instead of executing her.''

''She deserved neither,'' Alaric said, frowning. ''She was not at fault.''

''Of course not,'' said his mother, ''but we could

not allow her to spread tales among the populace. The power is best used when secretly used."

"I have tried to use it as little as possible. A reputation for magic is not one I ever desired."

"You could have been very rich," said the Baron.

"I could have been very dead as well. In some countries, magic is not looked upon so casually as here."

Lorenta nodded to her husband. "He has been wise."

"He has at least been careful—that is a virtue worth possessing."

"Come, Alaric," she said, drawing him toward the doorway. "Let us return to comfort downstairs and relax with a cup or two of wine, and you can tell us of your life far from Garlenon. You were found on a hillside, you said. . . ."

Sitting on the dais steps, he spoke at length of his foster parents, his childhood, his discovery of Dall and his wanderings after Dall's death, but he omitted a few personal details: Solinde, his exile from Royale, and Mizella; those things strangers—even though they be parents—had no claim upon. The hall filled slowly, some family members appearing from air at the tables, each behind a chair in which he then seated himself, others—mainly youngsters—walking in through the doorway to claim their seats. Soon his audience numbered near a hundred. Alaric marveled at their silence, their attentiveness, their familial resemblance. At last, he interrupted his reminiscence just after his meeting with Artuva in the well to say, "I've never seen my face in a good mirror, and now I know I will never need to."

A few of the older people smiled, and Dejarnemir, who stood at the edge of the dais, laughed quietly. She stepped forward, inclined her head toward the Baron, and said, "With your permission, lord." He waved a hand, and she vanished, to reappear in the same spot almost instantly, bearing a silver-backed oval mirror. Leaning toward Alaric, she held it up before his eyes.

He had seen his face in still pools of water, in the highly polished surfaces of copper pots, in the smooth wooden sheen of his lute, but now he knew that he had never really seen his face at all.

"You shave well," said Dejarnemir, "for a man who has no good mirror."

Alaric touched his own cheek, traced the line of his nose, the cut of his chin, the angle of his brows; then he turned his gaze to the Baron and his wife and saw his own features in theirs, but not in theirs alone. Any middle-aged man in the room could be his father, any matron his mother, any youth his brother, any maiden his sister. He had seen them as a family from the first—now he saw himself among them.

He glanced at the glass, at Dejarnemir, who held it steady before him. "You are my cousin," he said.

"We are all your cousins." She began to introduce the throng, naming names for row on row of similar faces, and Alaric marveled that she could distinguish one from the other. He let the names flow through his mind like water. Later there would be time to meet them as individuals.

"Now," said the Baron, when almost half the group had greeted their new relative, "I think we will show cousin Alaric exactly why he was turned away from our gate this morning. Clohelet, you may lead 'Fairy Gifts of Silver and Gold.' "

A young woman of about Dejarnemir's age moved away from her chair to stand in the center of the room;

all those similar faces turned in her direction as she raised her hands, palms outward, fingers stiffly spread. The crowd fell silent on an indrawn breath.

Clohelet gestured sharply, and suddenly the hall rang with song.

Alaric was astonished. He had heard the children sing their merry round, but that display bore only a remote resemblance to this chorus. The House of Garlenon had divided into four-part harmony, male voices against female, high voices against low, and the whole was a majestic sound like all the minstrels in the world gathered under one roof. No instruments accompanied them, but the women were flutes and harps enough, the men drums and deep horns. The sound swelled, faded, whispered or roared at Clohelet's gesture— a human instrument obedient to her slightest whim. Even the Baron himself and his consort followed Clohelet's direction as she shaped their music in the air.

And in spite of the multitude of voices, the words were clear and crisp:

> "Fairy gifts of silver and gold
> I bring my lady tonight,
> And if they turn to dross at dawn,
> What care I, for I'll be gone,
> To woo the next with a pretty song
> And fairy silver bright. . . ."

Alaric listened, entranced, the only person in the room not singing. When the music was done, he looked down at the lute which he had carried through the castle on his back and which now rested on the floor at his feet, and he thought about his own arrogance, his pride in his voice and fingers. He felt very small.

"But now you must show us your wares," said the Baron.

Alaric shook his head. "It's a poor show compared with what I have just heard."

"Ah, we warble singly as well as in large groups. If you've a song we haven't heard already, we'll listen gladly and take it as our own."

Alaric sang, but only half-heartedly, of a dragon-slaying knight and the fair princess he married. His voice sounded hollow to his own ears, as if he were in a vaster room, an empty room. His audience sat as silent and attentive as during the tale of his life, and afterward, they turned to each other and murmured quietly.

"Your voice is true," said the Baron, "but I think we have stolen the fullness from it. I apologize. I should have asked you to sing first."

"I would rather listen," said Alaric.

"You must join us," the Baron told him. "We melt together in chorus, and no singer can hear his own voice but only those surrounding him. There lies the true joy of song, not in mere listening."

"It is . . . an experience I have never known."

"Your age-mates can train you in a song or two so that you may discover it. Dejarnemir, come to me."

She obeyed.

"He is your charge. Teach him. And find him some new clothes." A gust of air accompanied his disappearance.

"Come, cousin," said Dejarnemir, "and meet your age-mates."

His mother nodded, and then she, too, vanished.

The young people were clustered at a table near the stairway. Clohelet was there—she who had led the chorus so artfully—and another cast in the same mold: Nidida. The rest were Bralion, Feronak, and Sarel, all youths in the first flush of manhood. Alaric searched their faces for the subtle details that would enable him to tell them one from the other.

"We have our differences, cousin," said Bralion, openly returning Alaric's stare.

"How came such intense resemblance in so large a family?" the minstrel asked.

Bralion shrugged. "For ten generations, no Garlenon has married outside the House."

"Truly?"

Dejarnemir said, "It was ten generations ago that the first Baron Garlenon discovered in himself the power of instantaneous travel. Desiring to cultivate it in his heirs, he married his cousin, arranged cousin marriages for his children, and so on, till we are all cousins now. And we all have that same power."

Alaric looked from one face to another. "You are my cousins. . . . Have I brothers and sisters as well?"

"Brothers and sisters, parents and children, all are cousins," said Dejarnemir. "The Baron, your father, is the son of your mother's father's sister and your mother's mother's brother, and therefore your cousin. The genealogy is far more complex than that, of course, but I'll leave it there for now."

Alaric shook his head. "How can you remember such intricacies of relationship?"

"We live with them every day. In this case, however, I'll admit that I am more personally interested than most. He is my father, too, and Bralion's."

"You are my sister," Alaric said, and he glanced from her face to Bralion's, saw the same resemblance there that he saw in the rest of the room, no more, no less.

"Two other siblings belong to a younger age group, one to an elder," she said.

"He will be the next head of tne House," added Bralion. "You'll see him seated beside the Baron at supper. He has a beard."

"In my foster home," Alaric said softly, "I had neither brother nor sister." He thought of Mira, his foster mother, who had made his childhood less than completely lonely by keeping him ever at her side. The other children of the village shunned him or even threw stones, and their parents dragged them indoors if he happened to pass by; they feared his mysterious origins. His foster father, too, knew such fear, and it turned him to violence when Mira was no longer alive to command his actions. It was then that Alaric discovered the greater loneliness, if greater safety, of a feral life in the woods; at seventeen it shamed him to recall that he had hardly been human by the time Dall found him.

He gazed out over the crowd in Castle Garlenon—rich fabrics, gold, silver, and gems glinted in the lamplight; stewards—more family members—were just entering with trays of flatware and crystal for the evening meal. The one-room mud and thatch hut of his childhood was worlds away, the three stools that were its only furniture, the gray wool homespun that had clothed him winter and summer, the porridge breakfasts and suppers spiced but rarely with a slab or two of tough old mutton. *Oh, if my infant heart had known what it was forsaking!*

"This is your chair," said Dejarnemir, leaning on the high slatted back. "Remember well the area immediately behind it, for that is the only place in the main hall to which you may freely jump."

"Jump?"

"We call our power jumping. You may not jump to or from any other spot in this room without the Baron's special permission. And no one else may jump to your chair, nor may he walk behind it unless you are already seated."

Alaric said, "With so many people using this mode of travel in the castle, it does seem that some injury would result, perhaps from two arriving at the same place. . . ."

"We follow certain simple rules. We walk close to the corridor walls—the center is reserved for short-distance jumping; we never jump blindly round a corner; we never jump to the intersection of two corridors; we have own customary places in each other's apartments and the common quarters. You'll learn. If you should entertain any doubts, someone will be nearby to instruct you. *Never guess.* Bralion, do you think you could find our new cousin proper attire for supper?"

"I could. I suppose we must walk to my rooms. Well, come along, cousin Alaric, and mark the route so that you'll not have to walk it more than once."

As they descended five flights of stairs, Alaric said, "I assume that the lady Dejarnemir did *not* go down to the city to fetch me on the chance that I might know a few new songs."

"You assume correctly. The guards reported your petition for entry—and your uncanny appearance. One Garlenon knows another, after all, even if he's never seen him before. The Baroness thought of the lost babe and insisted upon seeing you herself."

"They should not have turned me away from the gate. I might have left the city."

"No, they should not have turned you away, but

they had their orders, and they honestly believed we needed no minstrel." He grinned at Alaric. "It's true enough, cousin, is it not?"

Alaric had to acknowledge that.

"They kept watch on the inn. Had you left for some other place, you would have been followed. The Baron and Baroness discussed the situation for some time— and in the end, *she* prevailed." He halted before an ebony door carved with hawks and rabbits. "Remember this spot; you'll be coming here often, I think." The door was unlocked.

A huge dog with red-gold fur greeted Bralion as he entered, ran about and between his legs, reared up to place great paws on his chest, and licked his face. "This is Delf. Delf, this is your new cousin, Alaric."

Alaric let the dog sniff him, then stroked the sleek fur. "Even the dog is a cousin?"

"Informally," said Bralion, and he pushed the animal firmly aside and bade it lie down.

The room was furnished with large, comfortable chairs and heavy tables. The soot-blackened fireplace was cold but contained a thick bed of ash and fresh-laid logs and kindling; an oil lamp on the mantel provided illumination.

"Beyond the drapery," said Bralion, and he and Alaric passed into a small but opulent bedchamber. The bed was wide, covered with a green velvet comforter; the floor was hidden by a plush brown and green carpet; the walls were hung with tapestries of hunting scenes, with swords, bows, and arrows, with horns, antlers, and tusks of every size.

Bralion swept a pile of cushions off the brass-bound chest at the foot of the bed. "Have you a color preference?" he asked as he tilted up the lid.

"No."

"Blue? Gray? Some of both, I think. Here, cousin, these will surely fit you." He tossed a brilliant blue brocade tunic and a pair of blue-gray hose to Alaric. "The boots go poorly with these; you might try some black buskins—not fit for much walking, but then, none of us walks if he can help it, eh?"

Alaric stripped off his travel-worn clothing, laying the lute gently aside on the bed. "I would have thought that the Baron's children would live in the keep."

"This chain will look good on that outfit." He held up a necklet of linked gold medallions. "Dejarnemir will probably take you to the tailor tomorrow." He closed the chest and sat on top of it while Alaric dressed. "The Baron has declared it her task to train you into the family, but *I* will take the liberty of advising you thus, Alaric: we are all truly cousins. There are no special privileges here, no significance of rank or duty attached to sibship and parenthood. Feronak, for example, is as much the Baron's son as I, though he is not the Baron's son at all. We are all equal cousins."

"Except out eldest brother," Alaric said, slipping his feet into the soft velvet buskins.

"He showed an early aptitude, and now he is being trained for leadership. Someone must, and I for one am glad it is not me; I'd rather take orders than give them."

"So I call everyone cousin?"

Bralion nodded. "Everyone but the Baron and Baroness. They are lord and lady, at least until you are a few years older."

"Not . . . mother and father."

"No. Never."

"I see." Alaric donned the gold chain last, and Bralion helped him fit it to loops on the shoulders of his tunic.

"It's really quite simple. Now, let us return to the outer chamber and determine your jumping place." He held the draperies aside. "Ah, here, in the corner behind this chair. Mark it well."

"I mark it."

"Do you think you can jump to the hall?"

"Yes."

"Then I'll see you there. You can leave your old clothes; I'll have them washed with mine." He was gone.

Alaric turned back to the bedchamber for his lute. As he picked it up, his gaze fell upon one particular trophy on the far wall—the wide antlers of a buck red deer. Dall had shot a red deer once, he remembered, and they had traded most of the meat for silver at the nearest town. *Ah, Dall, I seem to have found some kind of home far from your grave, and far, too, from Royale.* Once more, he thought of Solinde, who had loved two minstrels and lost them both. Did she dream, in her wildest flights of fancy, that he came of a noble House?

No special privileges, Bralion had said; Alaric was just one more cousin, bound like the others to obey the Baron as liege lord. He wondered what the Baron would say to a marriage outside the House in the eleventh generation.

He looked down at his borrowed clothing. The court of Royale would hardly know him in such garb.

His stomach reminded him of supper, and he jumped to the hall. His age mates were seated already—he recognized them by their clothing: Dejarnemir in her black gown with the Baron's red chevrons across breast and back, Bralion beside her in blue, Feronak in scar-

let, Nidida in green and white, Sarel in yellow, and
Clohelet in pink and lavender. Their faces still looked
alike to him, though he thought he might have known
Dejarnemir in some other dress. She came forward to
take his arm and escort him to the table.

The Castle
Under the Hill

ALARIC'S FIRST SUPPER AT CASTLE GARLENON IN-cluded an array of foods and flavors that he had never tasted before: birds from cooler climes and fruits from warmer, vegetables of all colors, sauces sharp and mild, sweet and sour, hot and cold. He sampled everything, drank much good wine, and listened curiously to the table talk, which came primarily from members of an older generation.

"Killing the dog accomplished it," said one middle-aged man.

His neighbor disagreed. "It was an unnecessary risk. He had already been convinced."

"He didn't *say* he was convinced. He didn't *act* convinced."

"We didn't give him enough time. Another day or two and he would have come crawling to us."

"No, it was the dog. He couldn't imagine how it was done, save by magic. And when we told him *he* was next. . . ."

There were smiles all round the table at his unfinished sentence.

"Did you see the stones?" remarked a woman. "He has a fine gem cutter or two in his town. Perhaps they should be here instead."

Several cousins nodded, but one man said, "I believe the stones came from elsewhere."

"Well, we ought to find the source," said the woman.

"I don't doubt that we will."

Feronak spoke quietly, pitching his voice to reach only his nearby agemates. "Who's for a game?"

"I," said Sarel and Nidida, almost in unison.

Bralion, Dejarnemir, and Clohelet nodded agreement.

"My place?" suggested Feronak.

Bralion said, "No. Cousin Alaric doesn't know where it is. Let's say my sitting room. Shall we jump?" He disappeared, and instead of replying, the others disappeared, too.

Taken by surprise, Alaric found himself abruptly alone at the foot of the table. The older people ignored the mass exit and continued their conversation. Hastily gulping the last of his wine, Alaric jumped.

The others were already there, of course, waiting for him.

"Slow reflexes," said Feronak. "I suppose that's because you haven't done much jumping in your life in the Outlands." He sat on the floor stroking Bralion's red-gold dog.

"I've jumped now and then," replied Alaric, "but not regularly."

"You had a game in mind?" Bralion said to Feronak.

"I did indeed, and I propose it especially in honor of our new cousin—a round of Blind Man."

"Oho, vicious!" giggled Nidida.

"Exactly," said Feronak, crossing his arms over his chest and grinning so broadly that his cheeks seemed likely to burst.

"Hardly fair," said Bralion. "I don't think he can tell us apart yet with his eyes *open.*"

"Oh, come now, cousin. He surely has the Garlenon memory. I'll wager he does well enough."

"How much will you wager?" asked Bralion.

Feronak looked to Alaric, considered him with narrowed eyes and furrowed brow. "Three nights," he said at last.

"Elvala, isn't it?"

"You know it is, cousin. It's been her for months."

"Quite a wager, cousin. I think you're a bit too sure. Unless, of course, you're tiring of the lady."

"Will you accept the wager?"

"What can I offer of equal value . . . if I don't know the value of *your* offer?" When Feronak made no reply, Bralion said, "Very well. If I lose, I'll take your gate watch for three days. Will that do?"

Feronak exhaled a long breath. "That will do excellently."

"Does someone have a blindfold? Clohelet, your kerchief."

She drew a turquoise silk from her sleeve and passed it to Bralion.

"Come, cousin Alaric," he said. "Now we must wind this bandage about your eyes and administer our own test of your authenticity. This one, however, will not put your life in jeopardy."

"What manner of sport is this?" asked Alaric.

"A child's game," Fenonak replied. "One we play often as we grow into our power, for we can't cheat at it. When your eyes are sealed, we spin you round till you nearly fall over with dizziness, then we move about the room to further confuse you. Blinded, you must locate one of us and identify by touch alone."

"And you mustn't be sick," Nidida said. "If you get sick, you lose immediately."

"Hush, Nidida," said Dejarnemir.

"I fear you'll lose your wager, cousin Feronak," said Alaric.

Feronak shrugged. "If I were always sure of the outcome, I would never bother gambling."

"Now the bandage," said Bralion, and he wrapped the silk round and round Alaric's head until all vestiges of light were blotted out. "And now the spin." He took Alaric by the shoulders and turned and turned and turned . . . until Alaric cried halt.

"I will be sick if this goes on, and much as I wish to please my cousin Nidida, I do not care to spoil the carpet."

Bralion stepped away, and Alaric staggered a moment before drawing himself up straight. The darkness of his mind still whirled, and his stomach was none too comfortable. "I can remember spinning like a top as a child, for the pure joy of it, but I haven't done so in years, and now I know why. Oh, who would wish to play any game after such an experience?"

No one answered him, and he listened closely to the room, thinking that they might have all jumped away, that this whole diversion was actually a joke on him. But no, there was a barely suppressed giggle, there a quiet step, and there a long skirt brushing the rug. He waited till his sense of balance returned, and then moved forward slantwise, toward the last sound, his arms outstretched.

His right hand encountered smooth cloth molded over soft yielding flesh—a breast. "I believe I have found one of the ladies," he said. A masculine laugh erupted behind him, but the woman he touched made no sound. From that, he assumed she was not Nidida. "My apologies, cousin, but a blindfolded man is not responsible for any accidental breach of etiquette."

He felt of her head, her hair, the lines of her jaw and nose, and he knew they would not reveal her identity to his stranger's hands. Of her gown, however, he had a clear memory—it was not the loosely draping, puff-sleeved dress of Clohelet nor the low-necked, tight-waisted garb of Nidida. His fingers touched her shoulders and her back, located the seams that marked the positions of the two red chevrons.

"This is Dejarnemir," he said.

The silk was slipped away from his eyes, and he found himself gazing at her face.

She smiled. "Feronak has won his wager."

Behind him, Alaric heard Bralion give a mock sigh. "The fair Elvala must needs wait till some other time."

Feronak clapped his new cousin's shoulder. "Welcome, O true member of the House of Garlenon. This calls for wine. Bralion, as loser. . . ."

"Yes, as loser," said Bralion, and he vanished in search of a decanter, to return only a moment later.

"I am flattered," said Dejarnemir to Alaric, "that you remembered . . . the dress."

"In future, I will remember your face," he said.

Feronak passed him a glass of red wine. "Beyond the eastern forest where you have been—beyond the edge of the world, it would seem—what is it like there, cousin?"

Alaric sat down on a green velvet couch, and Feronak sat beside him. Bralion, Clohelet, Sarel, and Nidida found their own chairs and pulled them close. Dejarnemir transferred flame from the oil lamp above the mantel to the kindling on the hearth, then took a cushion near the new warmth.

"Beyond the eastern forest," said Alaric, "the world is much like it is here, but poorer. I have sung in great houses, in palaces, but none so rich as this." He laughed. "Little did I dream that I belonged in such a place." He raised his glass in a toast. "To the House of Garlenon—long may it prosper."

"Of course," said Bralion, and he drained his wine to the dregs. The others followed suit.

Alaric gazed at his glass, at the fine color of the liquid within. "This wine is excellent."

"It comes from a vineyard to the south," said Feronak. "The finest vineyard in the world."

"Well, the finest vineyard that we know," said Bralion.

"I go there every year to make certain that the entire crop is sent to us," said Feronak.

"And to keep the local vassal properly respectful," murmured Dejarnemir, prodding the fire with a long-handled poker.

"They don't give us much trouble there," Feronak replied. "That business with the younger son is hardly worth mentioning."

Dejarnemir drew a burning splint from the fire and blew it out like a candle. "What do you think the Baron will do with our new cousin?"

Feronak shrugged. "Put him on guard duty at the Second Gate perhaps. He's not trained beyond that. He'll have to take lessons with the younger age-group."

"I don't think so," said Dejarnemir.

"Oh, he will take lessons," said Bralion. "The Baron wouldn't omit that, but I understand your meaning: cousin Alaric has vast knowledge of the Outlands. The Baron won't waste that knowledge on guard duty."

"You're going to have a special place in the household someday, cousin Alaric," said Dejarnemir. "Special duties and special obligations."

"I will rely on your assistance."

"I see great times ahead for the House of Garlenon."

"I see hard work," said Bralion. "Sometimes I wish we could leave off conquering new lands and stay as we are now."

"Don't let the Baron hear that," said Feronak.

"He knows of my laziness, and he knows, too, that I always follow orders." His fingers turned his wine glass slowly, feeling of its intricately etched design. "I am allowed to have my own thoughts and desires; we are all allowed that."

"You could retire to an estate," said Feronak.

"What, and leave you to dice alone, cousin? No, I'll stay and do my share. It's well that someone else will be the next Baron, though, for I have no ambition beyond this wine, these clothes, this furniture. What can the rest of the world give us that would be better yet?"

"We won't know until we go there," said Dejarnemir. "Furs, spices, gems of some new color. I've heard that somewhere to the east are folk with yellow skin and slanted eyes. Is this true, cousin Alaric?"

"Not to my knowledge. Unless they live much farther east than my home."

"Your former home," said Dejarnemir.

"Yes, my former home."

"Sing us a song, cousin; play that lute you carry with you everywhere."

Alaric smiled and glanced down at the lute, which lay within easy reach on the floor beside the couch. "I carry it everywhere because I lost my last one by leaving it behind me. Those villagers I told you of, the ones who put Artuva in the well—they couldn't burn me, so they burned my old lute instead."

"No need to fear that here."

"Habits stay with us long beyond their time of usefulness." He picked up the instrument, strummed a chord. "But where can I leave it with confidence?

Surely not in the hall, where curious children and curious adults might accidentally damage it.''

Bralion cleared his throat. "He has a room, has he not?''

"He has a room,'' said Dejarnemir. "Lidia and Moiran are cleaning it and hanging fresh curtains; they promised it would be ready later tonight. You see, cousin Alaric, the House of Garlenon will not condemn you to sleep on the floor of the hall.''

"I have slept in less comfortable places.''

"Cousin, sing for us,'' she said.

He plucked a single string. "You were to teach me to be a member of the chorus.''

"That can come later. Now, this moment, sing us one of your favorite songs.''

"One of my favorites?''

"Yes.''

He thought back, back to his days with Dall—their wanderers' life in Bedham Forest, the castle that had been their goal, the woman . . . he saw her in his mind's eye as that first time: her green eyes, her long dark hair caught in a white lace net, her green linen gown girdled with a gold chain. He had gazed at her long, and then the King her father had asked for music.

> "Upon the shore of the Northern Sea
> Stands a tower of mystery,
> Long abandoned, long alone,
> Built of weary desert stone
> For a purpose now unknown. . . ."

As he sang, his thoughts roamed through those days, through the mornings of fumbling swordplay and the sweet afternoons with Solinde. His gathered cousins seemed to fade, their attentive faces becoming insubstantial, overlaid with scenes of memory. He hardly noticed when the song finished; his fingers continued to play over the lute strings long after his voice had ceased.

"He's a fine addition to the family," Dejarnemir said. "The Baron heard only a shadow of our new cousin's voice."

Alaric's eyes focused suddenly on his surroundings: Bralion's room, the fire, Dejarnemir at his feet. "I thank you, cousin. My mind was elsewhere for a moment, thinking of the last time I sang that song, far away, far away. . . ."

"Not far for one of us," said Feronak.

"No, perhaps not for one of us." He glanced at Feronak, then at Bralion and Dejarnemir—they seemed to be the eldest of the group, older than he by three or four years. He wondered if any of them were married. Feronak? No, Elvala must be a mistress; one did not barter one's wife for a wager. In ten generations, Dejarnemir had said, no Garlenon had wed outside the House. Was it only custom now, or was it still the Baron's law? He wanted to ask, but not while all of them listened.

Feronak drew a pair of dice from the pocket of his tunic, sat back, and tossed them from hand to hand. "You have the board and pieces, I believe," he said to Bralion.

"Another game to teach our new cousin," said Bralion, and he grinned as he rose to fetch it from the cabinet on the far side of the room.

The board, a large polyhedron of inlaid diamond shapes in three different shades of wood, was laid on a low table. Small metal disks, enameled in various bright colors, were passed around, several of a single hue for each player.

"Dejarnemir always wins," said Nidida, thrusting her lower lip forward in a pout.

"You don't have to play if you don't want to," said Feronak.

Nidida placed three of her tokens on the board.

"The idea is to capture all the other pieces and to finish at the central diamond," said Bralion, and he proceeded to maneuver his own tokens and to teach Alaric the complex game of skill and chance called Kemdon, while the others played against them both in earnest.

A long time later, when he had at last begun to absorb the multitude of rules and was almost ready to continue without Bralion's assistance, Alaric was swept off the board.

"Sorry, cousin," Bralion said. "She really is quite good." Only a few moves later, he saw his own men—the last obstacles between Dejarnemir and the central diamond—eliminated.

"You need more practice," said Dejarnemir. "And a little wager would enliven the game."

"I won't bet against you, cousin."

"Nor I," added Feronak.

"Then I suppose we must find a new game I haven't yet mastered."

Bralion shrugged. "I see a great player in our new cousin. Perhaps he and I and Feronak can practice without you and manage some kind of surprise someday."

"I look forward to it."

Bralion glanced at Alaric. "She plays with the Baron when she wants a *real* challenge."

Alaric rubbed his eyes. "This is the sort of game that could last till dawn."

"Oh, there have been times," said Feronak, "when I've given our cousin Dejarnemir a race."

"You did well tonight, Feronak," she told him. "I would like to see you pitted against some of the older players."

"And what of me?" said Bralion in mock arrogance.

"You are too lazy," she said. "Come, cousins, I think our new relative would wish to be shown his bed at this time. I'll see if it's ready." She vanished, reappeared. "Yes, it's quite ready."

"As am I," said Alaric, stifling a yawn. "I woke early this morning."

"I'll show the way."

"Will you come back after?" asked Bralion.

Dejarnemir shrugged. "I have a few matters to look into."

"Feronak and I will be here, and whoever else wishes to stay."

Out in the corridor, she said, "You're not far from Bralion, just a few doors away. The room has been unoccupied for some months, but our kind cousins have made it habitable for you; they even laid a fire."

The door was carved with winged dragons and gilded along their scales and forked tongues. Dejarnemir turned the brass handle.

"Is there a key?" asked Alaric.

"No. What lock could keep us out?"

"I mean, strangers, visitors."

"Strangers are not allowed within the Second Wall."

The room was large and luxurious: a plush green carpet covered the entire floor save for a stone crescent before the cheerfully blazing hearth; a thick blue velvet comforter hid the sheets of the wide bed; deep green curtains framed a narrow window, let in the cool night air. An upholstered divan was set by the fire, and a brass-bound trunk piled high with multicolored cushions served as a second couch.

Lying on the cushions was a familiar bundle—Alaric's bedroll. He unfolded it. His meager belongings were all there; an empty knapsack, a crust of stale bread, a cake of soap, a razor, and the sword. He lifted the sword, pulled it free of its scabbard, and gazed at the blade.

"There's a fine weapon for a poor minstrel," said Dejarnemir. "Why do you not wear it instead of leaving it wrapped in your blanket?"

"A minstrel with a sword is a walking contradiction," he replied, and he propped the weapon and its sheath on the fireplace mantel. "Let us call it a trophy. My only trophy." He indicated the blank wall above the hearth. "In Bralion's bedchamber, this wall is quite crowded."

Dejarnemir smiled. "The trophies and weapons are Bralion's own. If you want a few, you'll have to hunt with him. My walls are hung with fine weaving from the south, scenes of waterfalls and forest glens, and with round plates of beaten gold cleverly embossed and inlaid with gems. There is a broad choice of ornamentation in the storerooms."

Alaric set his lute in the trunk, then relaxed on the divan, his feet propped up on cushions. "Now that I have a room of my own, I suppose I am an official member of the family."

Dejarnemir knelt on a large pillow on the floor, her feet tucked under the long skirt of her black and red gown. "You were a member the moment you passed the test."

"The test . . . would the Baron truly have left me in that sealed room to die if I had failed?"

"Yes."

He grimaced. "That is . . . grotesque."

"We must all pass the same test when we come of age to have the power."

"And the ones who fail. . . . ?"

"They were weeded out long ago. The strain is strong now, after ten generations, and the test has been a mere formality for over a century."

"Dejarnemir, you've been bred like cattle, like dogs, for that one trait!"

She gazed serenely into the fire. "You think to revolt me by that comparison, but you do not. We know what we are, and we are proud of our heritage."

Leaning back, he studied the flickering play of shadows on the ceiling. "Now that I am a Garlenon . . . will I be expected to wed within the family, too?"

She glanced at him. "Of course."

"Is there no way of avoiding it?"

"Do we all repel you so?"

"No, it isn't that."

"Then there is someone else. Perhaps . . . you are married already?"

"No, I am not married. But there was a girl, a highborn girl. As a poor minstrel, I could not approach her."

"And you are thinking, a baron's son is quite a different thing from a poor minstrel."

He turned on one elbow to look at her. "Yes."

Dejarnemir rose, walked the length of the room and stopped at the window to look out at the stars. "How long since you've seen her?"

"Two years."

"Two years is a long time. Are you sure you still want her?"

"I am sure."

"Perhaps she is wed to someone else, someone of a proper station."

"No!" His own shout startled him, and he took a

deep breath before continuing in a more controlled
tone, "No, I think not. She is only sixteen."

"A high-born girl, perhaps an only daughter with a
sizable dowry?"

"A king's daughter."

"Ah . . . they tend to marry early. Have you never
attempted to find out?"

He shook his head. "I was exiled on pain of death
for desiring her. I have never dared return."

"It would be a simple matter to steal her."

"A king's daughter deserves better."

"Better than a life at Garlenon? There is none better, as well you know, cousin. Steal her and make her
your mistress."

"No, cousin. I would not offer less than marriage."

"Then you'll not have her at all."

"I'll speak to the Baron."

"He'll not give in."

"Not even for a long-lost son?"

She turned to look at him and leaned back against
the windowsill. "In seventeen years, he grew accustomed to loss of a cousin. A mere cousin. Don't think
that you are special, Alaric, simply because you are
the fruit of his body."

"And my special knowledge?"

"It will not bend him to your whim."

"What can he do to me if I disobey?"

Her gaze lowered, fixed on the carpet. "He can
make you a poor minstrel once more."

Alaric sighed.

"Life at Garlenon is sweet," Dejarnemir said softly.
"But we must pay for that sweetness."

"Have you ever been in love, Dejarnemir?"

"I think so."

"With someone you could not have?"

After long hesitation, she spoke stiffly. "It is not

considered good manners to question a cousin so closely about his private life.''

Alaric sat up. ''Forgive me, cousin. I only wondered . . . what do the folk of Garlenon do when they love outsiders?''

''The men take mistresses, give them ruby pendants and red houses within the Third Wall. Occasionally, a woman will find a lover in the city. But Garlenon children must be of pure blood, they must possess the power.''

''And if a cousin loves no other of the family. . . .''

''We have our duty, cousin, our payment to the House.''

''Yes,'' he said. ''I suppose I must pay for this room, these clothes. . . .'' His hands clenched into fists. ''I am no nearer to her now than I was as a minstrel.''

Dejarnemir came close to the divan, stood over him. ''In two years you have not seen her, Alaric, or heard her voice. It's a memory that you love, not a woman of flesh and blood.''

He looked up at her. ''Perhaps there is some truth in what you say.''

''Memories, dreams—they are a poor substitute for reality.'' She sat down on the edge of the couch. ''Touch me.''

He stroked her cheek with one finger.

''No, here.'' She pulled his hand down to her breast. ''During the game . . . I stood where you had to touch me first.''

''Dejarnemir—''

She pressed his fingers, trapping them with her own. ''When I journey into the city, the men look at me, and not merely because I wear the Baron's colors.''

''You're very pretty, I cannot deny it, but you're also

my sister. I never had a sister before, but I know this
is not proper. . . ."

She leaned close till he could feel her warm breath
on his cheek. "It is proper here, cousin, quite
proper." Her hands slid up along his arms and crossed
behind his neck. "Surely you need no instruction in
this," she whispered.

He smoothed her hair. "I know nothing of your cus-
toms, Dejarnemir. Will this bind me to you?"

She smiled. "Only as we are already bound, cousin
to cousin."

"Are you married?"

"No, but neither am I a virgin, if that concerns
you."

"What if . . . ?"

"I've borne one child to the family already; I am
not afraid of another. So many questions, cousin!"
She searched his face, her eyes wide. "Do you prefer
that I leave?"

"No." His hand still cupped her breast; now he
moved it to her waist, to her hip. "I have learned
caution in these last few years, Dejarnemir; it is a
habit not easily discarded."

"A valuable habit," she murmured, "under some
circumstances. Will you kiss me, cousin?"

His lips met hers, gently at first, savoring the wine
taste of her mouth, and then more firmly as her hands
moved upon him, as their bodies touched at full length.
Briefly, he thought of Solinde, and of Mizella, and
then he knew only Dejarnemir and the firelight dancing in her dark hair.

He woke, shivering, to a cold dawn filtered dimly
through dense curtains. The fire had burnt out, leaving
a thick bed of gray ash on the hearth. For a moment,
half-asleep, he could not recall where he was or who

lay in his arms, her face veiled by dusky tresses; not
Mizella, he was sure, nor Solinde who lived only in
his dreams. Then he saw the red and black gown on
the floor beside the divan.

She stirred in response to his small waking movement, and without opening her eyes she caressed his
naked flesh. "The bed would be warmer," she whispered.

Under the velvet coverlet, they clung together till
midmorning.

Dejarnemir stretched, arching her body into a bow.
"You are different," she said. "Your gestures, your
tone of voice, the way you walk. Save for that unmistakable face, I would doubt you were a Garlenon."

"And the power," said Alaric.

"The power . . . could have sprung up somewhere
else, just as it did in the first Baron Garlenon."

"The other proofs—the bloody hand, my age—"

"No, no. I do not mean to question your identity.
But you have grown to manhood far from our influence. It is that quality . . . of the foreign that attracts
me so. And yet, I wonder how we will train you in our
ways."

"With love."

"With discipline," she replied, and she bounded
out of bed. "Come, cousin, we've missed breakfast
and will have to be content with hard-cooked eggs and
cold bread. What a start to your new life!"

He took her in his arms. "A fine start. I'm glad that
the Baron gave me into your care."

"So am I." She kissed him quickly, then broke
away. "I must bathe and change, dear cousin." She
threw the red and black gown over one shoulder. "The
next time you see me, it will be in something less
official than this."

"Official?"

"This is a uniform. We always wear our uniforms into the city. I'll take you to the tailor later on for a fitting. When you've dressed, jump to the kitchen. . . . Ah, no, jump to the hall and ask directions to the kitchen. Tell them to feed you. I'll meet you there shortly." She vanished.

In the corner of the room farthest from the door, beneath a mirror of fine glass, Alaric found a stand with pitcher and bowl, soap and towels. The pitcher was full, left so, he assumed, by the cousins who had readied his room; he poured some water and splashed his face. He thought of Dejarnemir, of her slim, lithe body, her soft lips, her skilled hands. Exile could be spent in worse places than a wide bed in the wealthiest castle in the world.

"I must forget Solinde eventually, I suppose," he told his reflection. He felt a sudden weakness in his legs and clutched at the stand for support. Her face seemed to take form in the mirror, her green eyes staring out at him from the depths of the glass, staring at him with great sadness, as on that last day he had seen her. *There is no way I can have you,* he thought. *There never was.* His throat tightened. *But in two years I have not forgotten, and in my life, I vow, I never will.*

"After all," he murmured, "she doesn't expect me to return."

In the kitchen, the cooks were family members, both men and women, all of middle age save for two apprentices studiously observing the dinner preparations. He cajoled an egg and a slice of warm raisin cake from the overseer and perched himself on an unused table to eat. Dejarnemir did arrive shortly, wearing a black and white gown of harlequin pattern that made her the most conspicuous person in the room.

"The tailor expects you immediately," she said,

snatching an egg from a tray of salad garnish. "Come along."

"Where are we going? Down into the city?"

"No, no, cousin; you mustn't go into the city without a uniform. That's what we'll be getting first."

The tailor, a cousin of an age to be Alaric's grandfather, lived near the gate of the Second Wall. His rooms were a shambles of racks and chests festooned with cloth and ribbon and lace, of metal pins and clips that made the bare stone floor a glinting web of silver strands. He sat in a low rocking chair by a window which looked over the courtyard, and he hummed to himself as he stitched.

"Cousin Lendel, we are here," said Dejarnemir.

He looked up, smiled, and put his work aside. "Welcome to the wanderer," he said, circling Alaric, measuring him with his eye. "Are those not cousin Bralion's shirt and hose?"

"They are, cousin," she said, "and Bralion must have them back as soon as possible."

"You have chosen a poor day, cousin." He inclined his head toward Alaric. "I assure you, cousin, my stock is not ordinarily in such a state, but a number of the ladies were here yesterday and neglected to leave things as they found them. However, I think we will be able to find a few fabrics that will please you. You have no uniform, I suppose."

"No."

"Easily rectified. Bralion's clothes fit you so well, we'll use his measurements." He searched among the litter on the table nearest his chair and found a quill, an inkpot, and a scrap of paper; he scribbled a note. "The shoulders shall be a trifle narrower, though. It will be ready tomorrow. Now, if you see anything that strikes your fancy, cousin. . . ."

Dejarnemir helped him select a brocade, a velvet,

and a satin for tunics, silk for hose, and green leather for shoes. He refused ribbons and other ornamentation. "Too rich for me yet; I am a man of simple tastes and must approach vast wealth with a slow step."

"Whatever you wish, cousin," she said, "though I must confess I like the way you look in gold. . . ." She touched the chain that Bralion had hung about his neck. "I could find you another like this."

Alaric shook his head. "Let me pay for my food and clothes and lodging first and later I will consider gold."

"Whatever you wish."

They bade the tailor farewell.

On the stairway, Alaric said, "I have seen cousins in the kitchen, cousins sweeping and scrubbing, and I understand that it must be so if the power is to be kept secret from the world; but cannot our clothes be made by seamstresses in the city?"

"They *are* made by seamstresses in the city. But we have always thought it best that none should know precisely how many cousins the House of Garlenon numbers, and therefore we do not go into the city to be fitted individually. Lendel measures the fabric, lays the design, and sends it out to be finished; occasionally, he sews the complete garment himself—as he did with this gown I am wearing, as he has done with much of the Baron's own clothing. He is far more expert than the city seamstresses." She looked at Alaric sidewise. "This is his means of payment, cousin. He is fortunate in loving it so well."

"He never stands guard duty?"

"No."

"Will I?"

"Almost all of the men do. But you must be trained first. You'll have a lesson this afternoon."

"A lesson in what?"

"In being a Garlenon."

The lesson began in the lowest cross-corridor within the Second Wall and was conducted by Veret, a man of middle years whose gray-shot beard and hair intensified his resemblance to the Baron. His class consisted of ten maids and youths of thirteen or fourteen, and Alaric.

"My apologies, cousin Alaric," Veret said, "if our exercises seem tedious to you. These others have only known their power a short time and must be schooled."

Alaric bowed formally. "I will endeavor to learn whatever I can, cousin."

Veret's objective was the memorization of every corner of the enclosed citadel not a private apartment: the keep, the corridors, the stairways, the common rooms. He trained the serious-faced youngsters to march in cadence, to jump in cadence, to jump on command, instantly, without even a questioning thought. He taught them to jump carrying daggers, carrying swords, carrying man-sized slabs of wood; he taught them to jump wearing voluminous cloaks without leaving a single thread behind.

"This group is doing well," he said to Alaric. "They took a heavy toll of cloth and metal before they learned a touch of discipline."

"They do very well," said Alaric. "I fear it will require a great deal of practice before I know the castle well enough to equal them."

"And a great deal of practice you shall have. The Baron has instructed that you come to me every afternoon until your skill is at the proper level."

"And then?"

"And then you will be assigned whatever duties the Baron pleases."

During a rest period, the youngsters played a game

of buffets. Armed with padded staves, they contended by pairs while their age-mates stood all around to shout encouragement. Circling, feinting, jumping without warning, they dueled. A vanishment would set the remaining combatant spinning like a top, in hopes of catching his opponent in that flicker of an eye before he struck from an unexpected quarter.

"You'll see the older ones do this occasionally," Veret told Alaric, "settling disputes." He raised his voice. "Very well, cousins—the lessons must resume."

Dejarnemir had gone off on errands of her own for the afternoon; she joined Alaric at the evening meal. "All that walking always exhausted me," she said. "Did he take you up to the room at the top of the keep?"

"He took me everywhere. I could jump within the Second Wall in my sleep. Do we learn the courtyard next?"

"No. Between the Second and Third Wall are some who do not belong to the family, so there we must walk and pretend to be as the rest of the world."

"They are only the various mistresses of men in the family. Surely they know all about—"

"No. Only the family knows. And Artuva."

He lifted his glass, feigning to scrutinize the gold filigree encircling it. "Artuva knows about *me,* not about the family."

She speared a steaming piece of meat with her knife and nibbled delicately at the juicy edges. "You brought her to the city with you."

"She brought me."

"Seventeen years ago, I am told, there were those who thought she should be slain for her knowledge."

"Last night the Baron seemed glad that he had spared her."

"Yes. He sent her a visitor soon after you passed the test."

He set the glass down sharply. "He did not harm her!"

"No. He merely told her that your life would be endangered by her wagging tongue. She feels very strongly toward you, cousin; she swore to tell no one about your power, not even her own sister. Apparently she has kept her own counsel these seventeen years."

"So she told me. She traveled mostly in lands where she dared not speak of magic, and in some where even the casting of fortune-sticks was looked upon with horror."

"How, then, did she live?"

"By midwifery."

"With only one hand?"

Alaric shrugged. "She lived. And she suffered. I hope she has done suffering now, cousin. I owe her a great deal."

"She owes you her life."

"She has paid me well enough. My first gold I will send to her."

"I doubt that she needs it; hers is a wealthy family."

"I thought they fell from favor because of what happened at my birth."

Dejarnemir nodded. "Their women had been our midwives for many years, and your birth marked the end of that tradition. But amassing great wealth does not really require the Baron's favor." She wiped her mouth with a lace-edged napkin. "Have you done eating, cousin?"

"I wish my belly had a greater capacity for this fine food, but yes, I am finished."

"Good. Bralion has suggested that we begin your musical training tonight."

"Well, my body is tired; we may as well tire my voice, too."

"I'll meet you in his apartment, then."

They found him in his bedchamber, dusting a set of antlers, the largest of his trophies. "Do you enjoy hunting, cousin?" he asked.

"I am a poor marksman," said Alaric, "which is why I always depended on my voice to earn my bread."

"I wonder," said Bralion, leaning against the wall, "if you would teach me that song, the one about the tower."

"I thought this was to be *my* lesson."

"An even exchange, cousin: 'Fairy Gifts of Silver and Gold' for your song."

"I'd call it a fair exchange indeed, save that my songs sound best when accompanied by a lute, and therefore I must teach you that as well."

"Bralion plays the lute," said Dejarnemir. "Not as beautifully as you, but he'd rather string a bow, but adequately."

"I play *at* the lute," said Bralion. "Many of us do. But I don't think there's a soul in the castle that can match your skill, cousin. Our musical energies are almost entirely directed toward the chorus."

"Very well," Alaric told him. He perched on the scroll-shaped arm of a brocade chair. "Our exchange shall be this: you will train me to the chorus, and I will train you as a lone minstrel. Who knows—perhaps someday we two can travel foreign lands together, trading our songs for hospitality as my master Dall and I were wont to do."

Bralion frowned. "I doubt the Baron would like that. We have our responsibilities."

"The future is always an unknown, cousin. This

castle could fall and we be forced to wander the world. A minstrel's life is better than a beggar's or a thief's."

"This castle will never fall!" cried Dejarnemir.

Alaric shrugged. "In my life I have learned that it is always best to be prepared for catastrophe."

Bralion took the seat opposite Alaric's. "I will learn for my own pleasure, cousin. As long as the power serves us, we need fear no catastrophe. Now the words to 'Fairy Gifts' are simple enough. . . ."

That evening sped, and twice or thrice a cousin—not always an agemate—stopped by to have a word with Bralion. When this happened the person did not appear in the room itself but came to the corridor outside and knocked on the door. Dejarnemir explained that this was only common courtesy, that one never jumped to another's room unless specifically invited.

He invited her, and she was not loath to accept the invitation.

Days passed, and he learned the byways of the castle, jumping in the interior and walking about in the open courtyard. He found Lightfoot well-cared-for and gaining weight in a huge stable of handsome horses. Feronak introduced him to the fair Elvala, a charming young woman, pale and blonde and blue-eyed, with the longest fingernails Alaric had ever seen—he remarked upon them, and later, in private, Feronak showed the narrow red welts they had recently wrought upon his back.

Bralion schooled him in archery in one of the wider corridors of the lowest level.

"Isn't this a trifle dangerous?" Alaric asked. "What if someone walked by at the wrong moment?"

Bralion laughed. "Have you not yet learned that we walk only when absolutely necessary? Don't worry, cousin. A number of us enjoy archery, and we always use this selfsame place for practice.''

"I fear I shall break a good many shafts against these walls, cousin. Dall my master tried to improve my aim with little success.''

Bralion laid an arm across his cousin's shoulder. "Will you yield yourself entirely to me in this matter?''

"Yes.''

"Then you shall improve.''

Bralion was a kind and patient teacher, setting Alaric's arms, his shoulders, his hands, sighting past his neck at the green target. Alaric broke a number of arrows against the walls and floor, but he hit the edge of the target once.

"I can see,'' said Bralion, "that we will not go boar hunting for a good many months.''

"I tried to warn you of my lack of proficiency.''

"Lack of practice, rather,'' said Bralion. "If you come here every day faithfully, you will improve, I promise it. And I'll come with you.''

"If you have arrows to waste.''

"We have thousands of arrows to waste, cousin. We'll go down to the storerooms for more. And we'll get you a gold chain there, too—your tunic looks too plain.''

"I don't need a gold chain, cousin.''

"Of course you do. I'll meet you there.''

"Wait! Where?''

"In the storerooms.''

"I don't know where they are.''

"You don't? Ah, I suppose you wouldn't.'' He grinned. "Veret has forgotten that you are new to the castle. Every child knows where the storerooms are. Jump to the first cross-corridor within the First Wall.''

Alaric jumped. Bralion was already there.

"You'll come here often enough when you begin your weapons-training. It will be soon, I'd say, judging from Veret's reports on your progress."

"I thought I had begun today."

Bralion cleared his throat noisily. "Archery is not included in weapons-training. It is merely a sport." He ambled down the hallway. "Here is the place we are looking for."

The door was of light wood, painted with a shield of the Baron's red and black arms. Beyond it, the room stretched farther than any Alaric had yet seen. To the left and right were barrels, bundles, stacks of black arrows fletched in scarlet. Against the walls stood racks of unstrung bows, and on the floor were bins of the leather pouches that protected the waxed linen strings. Armor was here, too, blazoned with the double red chevron, and bright swords with the pommels weighted by gold-set garnets. Lances, shields, suits of steel chain were hung along the walls, and large wood casks below them yielded black leather gauntlets and pennons with the common device.

Bralion selected a handful of arrows, slipped them into the quiver at his waist.

"Where are the men who use these swords and shields, and these lances?" Alaric asked. "I have seen no one sharpening his skill with any of these things, not in the corridors, not in the courtyard."

Bralion gestured toward the far end of the long room. "Yonder they practice in the morning, fourteen of our cousins. By their own choice, more as sport than otherwise. The Baron feels that few of us need to know the tedious martial arts of the Outlands."

"Yonder?" wondered Alaric, squinting the length of the room. "There's hardly space for combat in this clutter."

"Ah, come along," said Bralion, and he threaded

his way through rank on rank of weaponry, to a plain door of iron-banded oak. He pushed it open. "The tribute of dukes and princes and kings."

A short hallway gave into a high-vaulted cavern whose ceiling dripped age-old stalactites but whose floor had been leveled and covered with thick braided rugs. Here were chests and trays and velvet bags, urns and bowls and buckets of wealth: gold chains and silver; rings, bracelets and buckles set with gems; cut crystal and white porcelain; silk, satin, and cloth of gold. Oil lamps lit the array, oil lamps that stretched as far as the eye could see, into the depths of the hill.

"The practice room is not so nicely appointed," said Bralion. "It lies some distance by foot; I doubt that you would find it interesting. Well, here is the treasure of the House of Garlenon. Will you choose a chain now that you've seen how plentiful they are?"

Alaric turned slowly to see everything. "This is the plunder of centuries," he said.

"Another reason among many for allowing no strangers inside the Second Wall." He selected a gold chain with a ruby pendant, hefted it thoughtfully. "If ever you wish to take a mistress from the city or elsewhere, it is our custom to give the woman one of these and a red house within the Third Wall." He slipped the bauble into his quiver.

"Dejarnemir told me," said Alaric, gazing upward, estimating the distance to the roof. "We are actually inside the hill itself. How far does the cavern extend?"

"Quite far. I didn't think Dejarnemir would be so free with such information quite so soon. It seemed to me that she had her eye on you."

"Has it been fully explored, are there outlets beside this one?"

"What we use has been explored. Beyond that . . . there are many branching passageways, twists and turns that could bewilder even a Garlenon. The Baron says there is a lake at the bottom."

"Sometime . . . I should like to see it."

Bralion shrugged. "I've heard it is a very, very, very long walk."

"But one would not be required to walk *back.*"

"I'd rather hunt boar."

Alaric laughed. "Coming here all your life has spoiled you, cousin. The largest cave *I* ever saw before this day was an old bear den where I couldn't stand upright."

"Well, perhaps you could induce a few of the younger cousins to go with you. Don't go alone. The Baron has warned us strongly against roaming the caverns alone. In my great-grandsire's time a lone cousin was lost here, in spite of his power. They found the skeleton many years later."

"A grisly tale indeed. Well, there will be time and time to explore in future."

"This would look well on you," Bralion said, choosing a chain of gold and silver filigree ovals.

"I don't want it, cousin."

"Take it as my gift."

"What have I done to deserve it? I should be the one to gift *you.*"

"Then take it as from Dejarnemir. Surely you've done something for *her.*" He grinned. "She'd like to see you in a bit of wealth, cousin; gold attracts the ladies so. . . ."

Alaric gazed about at the treasure of the Garlenons. Its value was beyond estimate, beyond the worth of the whole of Royale, castle, country, and inhabitants. "Very well, cousin," he said, "since you have so much. . . ."

Bralion tossed the chain; it whirled in the air and slipped neatly over Alaric's head. "There's another sport I could teach you,'' he said, and they clapped shoulders, laughing together.

Dejarnemir shared Alaric's bed that night, and she smiled at Bralion's selection. ''I have one like it, as well he knows. This is his way of giving approval.''

''Approval of what?''

''Of whatever you and I might have in mind.''

He rose on one elbow, looked down into her face. ''What have you in mind, cousin?''

''At this moment, you.'' Her arms locked behind his back and pulled him close.

Veret soon considered his students ready for weapons-training. ''You may have watched some of your older cousins bashing each other with sword and mace, carrying about vast weights of armor and much-dented shields, and you may have thought that this sort of recreation might be amusing. In my opinion, it is not. In my opinion, it requires unnecessary exertion and is as likely as not to injure *all* parties involved. If you should care to train in such a pastime, you must petition one of those who already practices the art—though it is hardly worthy of *that* title. From me, you will learn the Garlenon mode of combat—as swift and sure as the flight of an eagle. You will begin by drawing your daggers.''

Every young cousin's belt bore a blade with hilt inlaid with gold or gems that flashed in the light of the oil lamps.

''As I call your names, you will jump to the common room in the fourth cross-corridor. There you will find a sack of cloth scraps roughly shaped like a man. You will stab it as if it were alive and then return here with all haste. I will be observing your every move.''

At random, he called their names, and as the youngsters vanished, he vanished, too.

So this is the army of Garlenon, Alaric thought. *Trained to come and go in an eyeblink, trained to pick off one opponent at a time, with no chance of harm to themselves.* He wondered how many years were required to make their maneuvers instinctive. *Even the girls.*

He kept pace, remembering all the while Artuva's tale of the siege of the castle in her grandmother's day: the enemy had fled after three nights of terror. Terror it would be indeed to be attacked by the hosts of Garlenon.

The youngsters learned their lessons thoroughly, stabbing sacks of cloth with great fervor.

"These are not men," said Veret. "We have no men to waste on your weapons-training. I now substitute the carcass of a hog for the sack. It is in the common room in the third cross-corridor. Alaric!"

Alaric jumped, found the carcass still warm from slaughter and bleeding only a little from the wound at the jugular. He stabbed it to the heart, felt the knife slip between two ribs in a manner wholly unlike the penetration of a bale of cloth. This sensation was unexpected after so much of the other, but not unfamiliar—he had dressed out game often enough in his wandering life. He jumped back to the group.

"Good," said Veret, and he called the next name.

Reluctantly, Alaric wiped his knife on a linen kerchief; he hated to spoil the fabric, but he hated more to leave his knife stained—his own knife, plain-hilted and nicked with use. He waited, alert, as Veret marked the rest of the group, vanishing with each to look over his shoulder. It seemed to Alaric that several of the youngsters took longer than necessary to complete their tasks.

Veret stood, arms akimbo, after everyone had

stabbed the hog. "Some of you have never worked in
the kitchen," he said. "Which ones?"

Three of the boys and one of the girls stepped forward, as did Alaric, but Veret waved him back.

"Today after your lessons, you four will report to
the cook and ask to be assigned to slaughtering. You
must learn to strike swiftly, without flinching. To all
of you, I say, this hog is not a man. But just as a hog
struggles at the slaughter, so does a man, and a man
usually has weapons at his disposal, and comrades in
arms. You must strike swiftly, you must be gone before anyone knows you have been present. Those of
you who do not heed my advice will surely die."

"We could wear armor," said one of the boys,
echoing aloud the thought that arose in Alaric's brain.

"Armor makes noise, even on the most graceful
dancer. Our art requires silence. If you wish to wear
armor, you are free to do so, but you will find it less
a help than a hindrance. That is all for today."

Alaric invited Bralion and Feronak to his room that
evening. He passed a flagon of wine and, without pre-
amble, he said, "I have never killed a man. Have either of you?"

Bralion's eyebrows lifted. "Ah, so Veret stole his
usual hog from the kitchen today!"

"Yes."

"Killing a hog is not like killing a man," said Feronak. "We ought to take slaves from some of the recent conquests—the ones that caused us trouble—and
give the children some real practice."

"Our cousin is just a trifle bloodthirsty today," Bralion said to Alaric. "The Baron has said he must return to the south for a conversation with the vassal who
lords our favorite vineyard. Life is not as quiet there
as it might be."

"He needs another lesson," said Feronak, frowning. "This time I won't bother coddling the boy."

"He left him hanging upside down from the highest branch of the tallest tree in the valley," said Bralion. "The boy's father must have had an exciting time bringing him down."

"Not half as exciting as he will this time, I vow."

"Cousins," said Alaric, "I asked—"

"Yes, of course I have!" said Feronak. "And so will you, once you've learned the knack of it."

Bralion pursed his lips, looked into his wine glass, and drank.

"I'm surprised you've lived so long without doing so before now," said Feronak.

Alaric turned his back to them, gazed into the fire. "There was a day . . . a moment . . . when I would have slain my master's killers. But there were two of them, and I was afraid. As a minstrel, I lived a peaceful life, attempting to give offense to no man." He lifted his eyes to the sword and its finely tooled leather scabbard, no longer representing wealth to a mind dazzled by gold . . . but still rich in memories. The blade bore a shallow nick where Trif the innkeeper had beaten his own blade against it. "I have always run away from danger. And now the House of Garlenon, my own house, asks me to change myself."

"We run away," said Bralion. "We are cowards one and all, afraid of death, and the power is our shield."

"Cousin!" cried Feronak, rising from his chair. "Those are ugly words!"

"But true ones nonetheless. Have you ever faced death, cousin? I have not, and I've killed my share of men. We are mighty because we run away. The power makes weakness our strength. Without it, we'd still be stewards in some great man's castle, as the first Baron

Garlenon was. He killed his master to gain a coronet—
and not in a fair fight. We Garlenon never fight fair.''

Feronak shook his head. ''Sometimes I don't know
why the Baron tolerates you, cousin. Your mood is
foul tonight.''

''As is yours. Why shouldn't the Baron tolerate me?
He knows my obedience is beyond question. But I
know what we are, cousin; I won't lie to myself.'' He
spoke to Alaric. ''You can ask to be set free of
weapons-training if you can find some other sort of
task you do well.''

''Like the tailor?'' murmured Alaric.

''Yes.''

Alaric shook his head. ''I sing and play the lute. I
see little point in offering those as alternatives.''

''Then you must change yourself,'' said Feronak.

''Then you must change yourself,'' said Bralion.

In silent agreement, they dropped the subject and
jumped to Bralion's room for a game of Kemdon.

On bright afternoons, after training, Alaric sometimes walked out in the city. He wore his red and black
uniform then—it was a rule of the House that no one
went abroad without the uniform, not even the small
children. Citizens shied away from him, jostling each
other in their efforts to let him move unobstructed;
where the streets had been near impassable to a be-
draggled young minstrel, they were now a narrow private highway to the man who wore two chevrons on a
field of black.

Often, he passed the inn where he had spent so many
hours after being turned away from the castle. Once,
he entered and ordered wine; the landlord did not seem
to recognize him, nor did the grizzled old man who
had engaged him in conversation on that long-gone
day. Alaric greeted them both with lifted cup, but they

returned his greeting with respectful bows and respectful distance; when he stared straight into their
eyes, their gazes slid away from his face, to the floor,
to the wall, to another person. He wondered if they
saw his face at all and not just the uniform. The at-
mosphere of the inn was not as he remembered it—
the clientele had quieted abruptly when he arrived. He
finished his wine and left quickly.

The courtyard was always cool—shaded by the high
Third Wall—no matter how hot the day. Alaric sat in
the grass beneath a tree and reviewed his latest stroll
through the city—he thought he knew the place well
enough now that he could jump almost anywhere in it.
Jumping was, of course, prohibited there, but he had
a craving for knowledge of his surroundings, in case
such knowledge were ever, for any remote reason,
necessary. And the city itself was fascinating, teeming
with vendors, craftsmen, fortune-tellers, tambourine
dancers, beggars dressed finer than many a rich man
in another land, and travelers from beyond the horizon
come with tribute for the Baron and tales of adventure
for any who would listen. Sometimes these last did not
notice the uniform, or perceive its meaning for a long
time.

Alaric was thinking quite seriously of questioning
the rule about uniforms; Dejarnemir explained that it
had a threefold purpose: first, to identify and command the respect due the House of Garlenon; second,
to keep the citizenry and the world at large from
knowing how many members the House numbered (the
great family resemblance precluded exact identifica-
tion of a family member by an outsider); and third, to
protect the wearer from the fruits of any anger he might
provoke by his actions in the city—the children in particular were safe from citizen retribution for the fre-
quent mischief they wrought among the flowers,

animals, and children of the city (a habit their elders
disapproved of but could not entirely discourage).

Alaric cared nothing for the respect due him as a
Garlenon, thought he could roam freely as he had arrived—a minstrel—and had no fear for his personal
safety in that guise. He was thinking of speaking to
the Baron about the matter when a woman approached
his tree.

"Hello, Alaric."

He lifted his eyes from the ground-sweeping green
skirt to the low-cut bodice and the ruby pendant dis-
played against bare flesh. An outsider, someone's mistress. The face was framed by dark hair.

Mizella.

"May I sit down?" she said.

He nodded, mute.

"You had not expected to see me here, I suppose."

"How long, Mizella, and . . . and who?"

"His name is Merevan."

An older cousin, Alaric thought, one he knew but
slightly.

"He came to the house to speak to Artuva the same
day you left. He saw me, and the next day he came
back. He was kind, well-mannered, really quite amusing. Not long after, he offered me this." She fingered
the pendant. "I didn't want to accept it. It seemed
such a great gift. I didn't know, then, what it meant.
He offered again . . . and I said yes. The next day a
litter came to take me to the castle, and now I have
my own red house and all the clothes and jewels I ever
desired." She smiled. "Far more than I had expected."

"You're pleased, then?"

"Yes. He's very nice, Alaric. And . . . he reminds
me of you. Older, but still. . . ." She folded her hands
in her lap. "How have you been, Alaric?"

"Well. Quite well."

"I see you're one of them." She touched the upper chevron on his chest.

"Yes. There was never any real doubt. . . ."

"You've seen your parents."

"Yes, though not very often."

She lowered her voice to a whisper. "They have it, don't they? They all have it?"

"Have what?"

"You know what I mean. I've heard the wild tales that the people in the city tell each other. The truth seems to be a well-kept secret—Merevan gave Artuva to believe that your life depended on her silence, but I think it's just that they don't want the truth to leak out."

"And your part in my return—what does Merevan know of it?"

"Nothing, I think. Artuva told him I was a recent companion, almost a stranger to you, that I was not a party to the secret."

"Then you must never tell him the truth," he murmured. "Nor anyone else."

"I won't. But Alaric . . . I'm glad you've found your own folk."

"Are you happy, Mizella? Is Merevan good to you?"

"Yes and yes."

"Do you love him?"

She shrugged. "I enjoy being with him, and he gives me anything I want. I'm luckier than most, Alaric—being barren, I'll never have to give up a child for him."

"Give up a child?"

"You must know that the children born inside the Third Wall are taken from their mothers."

"No, I didn't know that. What happens to them?"

"No one knows. Some say they're raised in the castle and taught their fathers' arts."

Alaric plucked a blade of grass, began to shred it with his fingernails. "The Baron has his rules. Those children would inherit the power; the secret would be out if they were left with their mothers."

"Does it really matter if the secret is out? Would that make the House of Garlenon any less powerful?"

"Mizella, we must not be overheard discussing such matters."

"Come to my house, then, and we can talk freely."

He shook his head. "It wouldn't be proper. I'll leave you now, Mizella, lest anyone think we are more friendly than we should be." He rose, offered a hand to help her up. "You *are* happy, aren't you?"

"Don't feel guilty about me, Alaric, I'm fine. Come visit me sometime. Bring a chaperone if you like." She smiled, let go his hand, and strolled away toward a table where three women sat over a game board.

He turned from her but saw her still in his mind's eye, and the past she represented. He had not thought of her for a long time, nor of his life before coming to Castle Garlenon. He had allowed Bralion and Feronak and Veret and Dejarnemir to fill his idle moments, especially Dejarnemir, her eyes and lips and arms. His days brimmed with new experiences, with sights and sounds and tastes, with lessons and games and dalliance, but his heart was empty. What he felt for Dejarnemir, he scarcely knew, but it was a pale thing beside his love for Solinde.

He waited long that evening in the corridor outside the Baron's private apartments, and at last, after countless cousins had passed in and out, he was admitted.

"Sit down, Alaric," said his liege lord. Swathed in a dressing gown of deepest purple velvet, he reclined on a gold brocade divan. At his elbow, a crystalline decanter betrayed pale amber contents; he lifted it in a cordial gesture. "Have a cup of wine. Veret tells me your progress is swift."

Alaric knelt on a plush footstool. "My lord, I am here to speak to you of matters pertaining to my future."

"Yes?" The Baron poured a tumbler of wine and proffered it.

Accepting the glass, Alaric drank to moisten his suddenly dry throat. "Matters which, I have been told, concern the House as well as myself."

"Your future and the House's future are one."

"I have been among you some time now. I have looked and listened; I've been given a great deal of advice. But there is something I must hear from your own lips, my lord."

"And that is. . . ."

"Whom must I marry?"

The Baron smiled. "You need not marry at all if you do not desire it."

"No, lord, that is not what I mean."

"You ask, then, if I have chosen your bride?"

"It is a fair question, lord."

"It is, indeed. Come back five years hence and ask again. You are too young to think of marriage."

Alaric drank once more and stared deep into the glass. "I have thought of it often."

"Have you?" The Baron's eyebrows rose. "And whom would *you* choose?"

"Of all the women in the world. . . ." He sighed, then straightened his shoulders and lifted his gaze to the Baron's face. "My lord, this is a time for plain speaking; must I wed within the House? I have been told this is the Baron's law, that none have disobeyed in ten generations."

"That is so."

"And I, too, must yield to it?"

"You must." The Baron smiled again. "But if you want her so much, an arrangement can be made for a red house in the courtyard."

Alaric looked down at the glass again, turned it slowly in his hands, and the lamplight flickered over its faceted sides. "I know. But she would never be allowed inside the Second Wall. She would be an outsider, a concubine, without position or title. Her family is noble . . . royal; they would never tolerate it."

"They could not prevent it."

"Dejarnemir thought the same." He rose from his footstool, set his glass beside the decanter, and bowed. "Thank you, lord, for allowing me this audience. My questions have been answered."

"Will you fetch her here, then?"

"No, lord. I'll leave her where she is. Good night."

He brooded some while, sitting by the fire in his room, torturing himself with visions of Solinde; and the greatest torture was the thought that if he went back to her for whatever reason, with whatever purpose, she might not remember him at all. Two years had slipped away, and in two years the world might turn upside down. For Alaric, it had done so indeed. When at last, in the dawn twilight, Dejarnemir knocked at his door, he was more than ready to forget the past with her.

Not many days after, the future enveloped him unexpectedly. He jumped to the hall for the regular evening session of choral song. His age-mates were there already, and the usual crowd of cousins, waiting to begin.

"I see I'm not late," he said to Dejarnemir, who sat with Bralion and the others at their table.

"Not for singing," she said. "That's going to be delayed. The Baron has some announcement to make."

"I think we're involved," said Bralion.

"Us?" said Alaric. "Have we done something?"

"We will. Better sharpen your knife."

The Baron stood behind his table, the Baroness to his left, the heir to his right. "Cousins!" he shouted, and the tumult of the throng ceased. "Cousins, the fortress at Brisenthal is besieged. Tomorrow, forty of us ride to save it. Let the following cousins take seats before me and be instructed."

"You see?" said Bralion when his name was called.

Alaric, Feronak, and Dejarnemir were also included.

"Women?" wondered Alaric, and he thought of the girls who were training with him under Veret.

"We are soldiers, too," said Dejarnemir.

The cousin in charge of the fortress at Brisenthal had jumped to Garlenon that afternoon to report the siege. Eight other cousins knew the route; they would guide their thirty-two companions on horseback. Five days of hard riding would bring them to a base some miles from the fortress. The plan of attack was simple: they would scout the besiegers' camp, jumping as near as possible, hiding behind trees and in bushes; they would locate all captains, their campfires, their tents, their beds; at midnight, they would jump to those beds, slay, and vanish. It was a well-worn plan that had never yet failed.

The forty were broken up into eight squads, each commanded by an older cousin of substantial experience. Alaric's commander was Veret himself. Bralion, Feronak, and Dejarnemir were on other squads.

"If all goes well," said the Baron, "our work will be over by this hour six days hence."

Alaric meditated through supper. He had never killed a man. He doubted he could bring himself to do so now. After the meal, he confided in Veret.

"The Baron says you must be blooded," Veret said. He clapped Alaric on the back. "There is nothing to be afraid of, you know. A Garlenon cannot be killed unless he's surprised, and in the middle of the night surprise will be on your side. Strike true and hard, then jump back to your base. For Garlenon, lad, remember that always."

Feronak and Bralion were gone when he turned to search for them. Dejarnemir caught his arm. "May I come to your room?" she asked.

"Yes, of course."

"Now."

He nodded, and a moment later they were both there.

She kindled a fire in the hearth. "You wondered what use that plain brown suit of clothes was that the tailor sent with the rest of your wardrobe."

"And you told me I'd find out eventually. And so I have. I wear it tomorrow. I hide in bushes or behind a tree in it. Ah, Dejarnemir!" He took her in his arms. "Must it be so soon? My training seems inadequate to the task."

"You'll do well, cousin. The Baron would not have chosen you for the trip if he had no confidence in you."

He loosed her long enough to lead her to the couch, and when they sat down he held her close. "What is Brisenthal, where, of what value? Who is besieging it and why?"

"I cannot answer all those questions, cousin. Lie back, put your head in my lap and relax." She stroked his hair. "Brisenthal is in the south, farther—much farther—than the petty fiefdom that Feronak bullies for wine. Brisenthal is on the very edge of the realm and vulnerable, you see, to attacks from the southern Outlands. We should have taken them ere this, but we delayed, and now one of them has made the first move against us. Eliander is the fellow's name—a count or some such, I'm not really sure. He besieges Brisenthal thinking he can beat us back; he disbelieves in our might. Now we must teach him to respect us."

"But *why* is he attacking? How can he hope to defeat a realm as far-flung and powerful as this?"

"He is attacking because he doesn't wish to pay us tribute. We had asked for a small sum, something he could easily afford, and he refused. I cannot guess why he thinks he can defeat us."

Alaric sat up. "Garlenon has been planning on conquering this Eliander's country?"

"Yes, but we've been busy elsewhere lately."

"Why don't we just leave him alone?"

"But cousin, he besieges Brisenthal. We cannot allow that!"

"Can't we come to some sort of agreement that would be satisfactory to both sides?"

Dejarnemir smiled. "Why should we? He will lose his country and his life, and we won't lose a single man."

Alaric leaned forward, elbows on his knees, chin propped up on his interlaced fingers. "How long ago did Brisenthal belong to someone else?"

She shrugged. "We acquired it when I was a child."

"And the rest—all conquered, I assume."

"Of course. Everything in this world is won by conquest."

"I think I begin to understand Bralion. Will it go on forever, Dejarnemir, beyond our lives, beyond our children's lives, till Garlenon rules the whole world?"

"Why not, cousin? That is a worthy dream for lords of power such as we."

"We must breed quickly, then; it will take a vast number of Garlenons to rule the world."

"Well, I am doing my share."

He straightened, turned to face her. "You're pregnant?"

"Probably."

He gripped her shoulder. "Then you must not go tomorrow!"

"I'll go."

"Too dangerous, Dejarnemir!"

"Nonsense. There won't be any danger at all. I've done this before. Several times."

"But not when you were pregnant?"

"No, but I'm not ill. I feel quite healthy."

"Does the Baron know?"

"No, and you shan't tell him. I'm not certain anyway. It's very soon to be certain. I merely suspect."

He looked into her eyes. "Is it my child?"

She returned his gaze levelly. "Yes."

He hugged her. "As the father of your child, I command you to stay here tomorrow."

"You may not command me, cousin. I will do as I like. And if you tell the Baron, I will deny it."

"You *want* to go?"

"Of course. I am a Garlenon and I do as my lord bids."

"How well trained you all are!" He shook his head. "I have not been here long enough, Dejarnemir. I'm an outsider, far more than the children of the red houses. From infancy they are part of the family."

She stiffened in his arms, drew back a little. "Who told you that we take children from the red houses and bring them into the family?"

"A woman in the courtyard," he said. "She spoke to me some days since, and the conversation turned to children."

"She was wrong," said Dejarnemir.

"In what way?"

"I told you we were a pure strain, cousin. Quite pure. No half-outsider has been allowed in the family."

"But they *are* Garlenon children. What happens to them?"

She looked toward the fire. "They probably would not pass the test anyway."

"Then. . . ."

"If the women have assumed the children are taken into the family, that is their foolishness. We make no promises."

"I see; they are killed."

"What is an outsider child? There are many such in the world."

Alaric leaned back, let his arms drop away from her. "I should have realized that only Garlenon is important."

"The women are warned that they cannot keep their babies. No one forces them to become mistresses of Garlenon men. They come to the red houses of their own free will."

He thought of Mizella and the two children she had abandoned because they were an inconvenience to her livelihood. He thought of the guilt and sorrow that plagued her memories. "It seems a high price. Do they lie to themselves because it is too high?"

"I am not lord of the House, cousin," she said softly, laying an arm across his shoulders. "Whatever I may think is not significant. I am a soldier, as you are. We must follow our lord's orders. Tomorrow, Alaric."

"Tomorrow." He gazed into the crackling flames. "I never thought to be a soldier." He looked up at the sword. "When Prince Jeris gave me that sword, he said I could sell it if I needed the money. Even he, who practiced single combat beside me in the court-yard of his father's castle, never expected me to become a soldier.'' He shook his head. ''Am I truly home?''

''You're tired, cousin. Come rest beside me.''

He let her lead him to the bed, and there he clung to her with his eyes closed. Later, he dreamed of blood.

He woke groggily when the quilts were ripped away and a dozen hands grabbed him roughly. For an instant, in the dim light of fading embers, he saw shadowy figures surrounding him, and then he was engulfed in chilly blackness. He reached out, clutched at emptiness, encountered a cold stone wall. Only his own breathing marred the silence.

He knew what had happened. Bralion was tolerated, his doubts outweighed by his innate loyalty to the family, but Alaric was an outsider, an unknown, full of questions and quibbles—he knew another way of life and could not be trusted to obey blindly. Fortunately, Alaric was a fool who would never suspect that his family might rid itself of him as easily as of a newborn babe or an enemy count.

Dejarnemir, perhaps, had betrayed him, or Bralion or Feronak, but no more than he had betrayed himself.

A group of them had jumped in cadence with him as their cargo—jumped to a cold, dark place that he had never seen. For the first time in his life, Alaric was trapped.

Already, he was feeling short of breath. It must be a small, tightly enclosed area, and the only fresh air it contained was that which the jumpers had brought in with their bodies. How long, he wondered, would it last?

He traced the outlines of his prison: four irregular stone walls encompassing a space not much greater in any dimension than the length of his body. In one corner, he encountered bones—the previous inhabitant. He shuddered, felt his stomach crawling up his throat; that some earlier prisoner perished here hardly boded well for this one.

Four blank walls, a blank floor, blank ceiling. He pounded on them with all his strength, and the sound indicated solid stone. That seemed unreasonable. In order to jump into this space, the Garlenons who had stolen him from his bed must have walked into it at some earlier time. One of the walls, at least, had to be artificial, brick or stone blocks sealed by mortar, pitch, or plaster. Closing his eyes for concentration, Alaric ran his fingertips across the face of each wall.

He breathed shallowly. An ache had begun in the back of his head, and his body felt heavy, as if he had run miles and were about to collapse from exhaustion. He wanted to lie down and rest for a moment, to lay his aching head on the icy floor, but he knew he dared not. Sleep would be the end of him; his would be the second skeleton in this tiny chamber. He wondered if there had ever been others.

He shook his head and opened his eyes to stare into the darkness—he felt less tired that way.

A cursory examination of each wall revealed nothing to his probing fingers. He swept over them again, more carefully, and found nothing but seamless natural stone.

His arms were heavy, he could hardly lift them, and, fighting the lethargy, he made a vast effort to stretch them above his head. His knuckles hit the ceiling while his elbows were still bent. Furious, he pushed upward, bracing his legs apart, till his body was taut as a bow and sweat trickled down his cheeks to chill him. He

screamed, and his voice was deafening in his own ears.
The darkness turned about him, as if he were once
more playing Blind Man with his age-mates; he could
almost conjure up Dejarnemir to stand before his
sightless eyes.

He fell over, and the sharp pain of his naked knees
striking the unyielding floor cleared his head. He stood
upright, touched the ceiling again, sliding his fingers
across the stone. Where wall and ceiling met, his nails
found cracks—his prison was a pit cut in solid rock,
topped by a single slab. Twenty or thirty men could
lift that cover, but one lone man would die beneath it.

His laboring lungs drew breath but found no suste-
nance. He guessed at the thickness of the ceiling, dou-
bled his guess.

And jumped.

His bare feet hit rock with a bone-jarring impact,
and he pitched forward. He had overestimated and appeared in midair. Darkness still surrounded him, but
he knew by the freshness of the air that he was outside
his tomb. He lay on the cold stone and breathed deeply.

At last, shivering, he climbed to his feet and turned
slowly, straining without success to pierce the blackness. He stretched his arms out to either side and
brushed no obstacles. He stepped forward, testing the
ground gingerly with his nearly numb toes. He had
not moved more than a few paces when he encountered an abrupt elevation in the floor—the base of a
stalagmite that rose and tapered to form an hourglass
with a stalactite depending from overhead. After Alaric had felt of the formation, he needed no further
proof that he was deep inside the hill, in the caverns.

He assumed the storerooms were near. He had no
rational reason to do so, for adequate torchlight would
facilitate short exploratory jumps, making any subter-
ranean distance an easy hike for a Garlenon, but he

made the assumption anyway for his peace of mind.
He knew he could not walk far; he was totally naked,
without any means of building a fire, and he could feel
the numbness creeping past his ankles. He could not
jump to warmth and safety, for he knew not where
they lay. That he had jumped out of his prison to a
destination calculated but unknown to direct experience astounded him—he was sure no other Garlenon
could do the same, and the skeleton he had left behind
was weighty evidence of that. But jumping out of the
cavern entirely was another matter; how far and in
what direction lay safety? He could not even guess.

And he was afraid to try.

The rough floor slanted neither up nor down. From
the echoes of his experimental whispers, Alaric judged
he was in a large room. He searched for a wall, found
one, and moved along it, following every twist and
turn. The floor made a sudden steep angle downward,
then up; the wall fell away to the left, then surrounded
him, alcovelike, and turned him back the way he had
come. He plodded ahead, scouting every step by touch;
he wanted to crawl on hands and knees, but every bit
of him that touched the chilling stone meant more of
his body heat flowing away. His calves were numb
now, he couldn't feel his lower legs at all. He thought
he was moving upward, but in the cold darkness his
sense of direction and his sense of balance were both
ebbing. He stumbled, sprawled, scrambled to his feet
and bumped his head on the wall. He ran in place for
a little while, trying to beat life back into his legs, and
when he was a trifle warmer, he resumed his trek. His
teeth were chattering violently, and the bumps that had
long since raised on his skin were thousands of tiny
points of pain.

How long he wandered, he did not know. Was it
morning already? Not a speck of light appeared to as-

suage the gloom. His stomach rumbled. His bladder begged relief, and he emptied it into the darkness. Somewhere above him, he was certain, the House of Garlenon was eating breakfast.

His forward foot skidded on something hard and cold and detached from the floor, but it was not a rock. Alaric stumbled, grabbed at the wall and saved his balance; then he bent to search for the object. His numb fingers awkwardly felt of a long hollow cylinder of metal, tapering to a point, rough-surfaced with rust—a torch-holder intended for wall mounting.

He was on a trail that other human beings had used.

He dropped the torch-holder and moved on, his left hand high now, sweeping the wall for other mounts. He found one where the wall turned at a sharp angle, another farther on, and then he stumbled again, this time over a rusty metal chest. The chest was empty, its lid flung back and hanging on a single hinge. Farther on, a second chest stood against the wall, also open, empty, and perforated by rust. Farther, there was litter underfoot almost constantly: old swords, a few dented shields, some pieces of armor, and other objects whose identity had been lost through years of slow disintegration.

Alaric wanted to cry out for joy, but he feared that unfriendly ears might hear him.

He felt the breeze. Light, evanescent, a mere breath across his trembling body. A cold breath. It blew from his back.

He turned, felt the breeze more strongly, for he had suddenly begun to sweat. He *knew* there was no way out behind, not for miles. He shivered more violently than ever and slapped himself for warmth. He thought of the hot summer sun that must have risen long since, the sun he had often tried to escape by lolling in the shade of the Third Wall. How could this cold breeze

come from the hot sun? He sniffed at it and smelled
no greenery, no dust of summer roads, only the cold
and damp. This was a breeze from the depths of the
earth.

He could not turn back. Therefore, he must believe
that as the breeze had an entrance to the caverns in the
depths of the earth, so it had an exit into the sunlight.
He resumed his walk.

His mind had long since begun conjuring sparks
from the darkness, worms of light that flashed across
his eyeballs and disappeared when he turned his head
to follow them, fountains of color, glowing balls, sheet
lightning. These lamps illuminated none of his surroundings, not even the wall beside his hand, and he
became slowly accustomed to ignoring them. Now he
saw a dim light far ahead, much like a number of dim
lights that he had observed during his time of dark
solitude. Previously, he had rejoiced and quickened
his pace, only to see the brightness fade at his approach and be snuffed out like a guttering candle. This
time he sighed and moved on at his customary pace
or perhaps a bit slower, for his legs, which had long
been without feeling, were nearly without strength as
well. He continued to knock into objects, but now he
did not stop to examine them. It sufficed that they were
there, mute guideposts, discarded against one wall of
a long corridor . . . or a series of rooms—Alaric had
ceased his attempts to locate the opposite wall.

He walked with his head down, morbidly certain
that when he looked up again the light would be gone.
He saw the texture of the floor change before his numb
feet felt it and only then did he comprehend that he
could see once more.

He ran, stumbled, fell to the carpet, and ran again.
He stopped when he realized he saw not the lamplight
of the storerooms but sunlight streaming through slit-

ted windows high overhead, illuminating a large round room built of stone by the hand of man. His entrance stirred up dust that floated, winking golden, in the sunshine.

He looked around, blinking, his mind fuzzy with exhaustion, his body still trembling with cold and the aftermath of fear. He saw walls partially covered by dusty, rotting tapestries. He saw a broad archway sealed by lowered portcullis and, immediately beyond, brick. He saw a stone staircase that circled the room, spiraling upward, passing beneath a matching spiral of windows. He went to the staircase, started up, found himself crawling on hands and knees. The stone of the stairs was neither warm nor cold to his limbs.

At the first window, he pulled himself upright to look out.

Low sunlight, but warm. He had been underground a full day. He leaned against the sill and let its stored warmth seep into his flesh. The city spread out before him. He was in the Castle Under the Hill.

Heedless of risk, he jumped to his bedchamber and found no one there, not even those who might be expected to linger for memory's sake. He stripped the bed, dug through the brass-bound chest, and made a bundle of his plainest castle clothes and two blankets, the sword and the lute. With fingers still half-frozen, he donned and laced his old minstrel's garments. Without a qualm, he flitted to the storeroom, secured a pouch of the Baron's gold, and returned to his room. Lightfoot, he feared, would have to be left behind.

Hoisting the pack to his shoulder, he made his silent farewells to the empty room, to Bralion and Dejarnemir, to Mizella and Artuva, to father and mother and birthplace. Then he jumped to a lonely grove of trees a few days' journey eastward. On a mossy spot between the gnarled roots of a large and venerable oak, he spread his pallet for the coming night. In the morning, he would move north, without horse or human comrade, a lute and a sword his only companions. Once again, he was merely a minstrel—not a baron's son, not a lord of power, but a wandering exile.